The BOY on the
BRIDGE

ALSO BY NATALIE STANDIFORD

Confessions of the Sullivan Sisters

How to Say Goodbye in Robot

The Secret Tree

The BOY on the BRIDGE

NATALIE STANDIFORD

SCHOLASTIC PRESS NEW YORK

Library of Congress Cataloging-in-Publication Data

Standiford, Natalie.
The boy on the bridge / Natalie Standiford. —1st ed.
p. cm.
Summary: It is 1982 and nineteen-year-old Laura Reid is spending a semester in Leningrad
studying Russian, but when she meets Alyosha she discovers the dissident Russia — a world
of wild parties, underground books and music, love, and constant danger.
ISBN 978-0-545-33481-5 (hardcover)
1. American students — Soviet Union — Juvenile fiction. 2. Saint Petersburg
(Russia) — Social life and customs — Juvenile fiction. 3. Soviet Union — Intellectual
life — 1970–1991 — Juvenile fiction. 4. Soviet Union — Social life and customs —
Juvenile fiction. [1. Foreign study — Fiction. 2. Dissenters — Fiction. 3. Saint Petersburg
(Russia) — Social life and customs — Fiction. 4. Saint Petersburg (Russia) — History —
20th century — Fiction. 5. Soviet Union — History — 1953–1985 — Fiction.] I. Title.
PZ7.S78627Boy 2013
813.54 — dc23
2012033037

10 9 8 7 6 5 4 3 2 1   13 14 15 16 17

Printed in the U.S.A.   23
First edition, August 2013

The text type was set in Requiem.
Book design by Kristina Iulo

FOR EDWARDO

1

★

GYPSIES ON THE BRIDGE

JANUARY 1982

*L*aura and her roommate Karen tramped along the frozen mud road that led through the university, past a wall with *OGNEOPASNO!* painted on it in huge red letters. An icy wind blew off the Neva River. It was January in Leningrad.

"Flammable," Karen mumbled, reflexively translating. Somewhere nearby, invisible to the naked eye, there was, apparently, a fire hazard.

"There's nothing to eat," Laura complained.

"What are you talking about, comrade?" Karen put on an exaggerated Russian accent. "The Soviet Union produces much food that is tasty. If you don't like fish head soup or unidentified gray meat, that is your problem. The gristle is the best part! Only four and a half months to go."

Laura's laugh was hollow. Two weeks in the Soviet Union and she was already anxious to go home. Five months of bitter cold, inedible food, filthy dorms, boring classes . . . how would she survive it?

"I wouldn't mind a little deprivation if everything wasn't so dull and *gray*. Where is the passion?" Laura moaned as the wind bit at her nose. "Where is the soul?" All she saw around her was ugliness and a depressing conformity. "Where is the beauty?"

"Is that what you came here for? I came for the wild punk-rock scene. You think *you're* disappointed. . . ." Karen stopped just outside the university gate. "I'm going to find a bakery or something. Loaf of black bread?"

"And some cheese, please," Laura requested.

"If I can find some."

On their second day in Leningrad, Karen and Laura had walked into a bakery and asked — in their careful classroom Russian — for two rolls. "Can't you see we're busy?" the stout woman behind the counter barked. She wore a white apron dusted with flour and a white kerchief in her hair. No one else was in the store except for a skinny, sullen teenage boy who slouched against the empty bread shelves.

"But . . . we are the only people here," Laura pointed out.

"Do you have any black bread?" Karen asked.

"We're busy!" the woman snapped.

Baffled, the two Americans left empty-handed. A few days later, when Laura had stopped in a meat shop to ask for some *kolbasa*, the butcher replied, "We're busy! Any idiot can see that!"

Again, she was the only customer in the store, but as she glanced around she realized that they had nothing in stock but a gray pile of ground pork.

"Shoo!" the butcher said. "I've got work to do." He snatched up a penknife and started picking his teeth with it. Laura left.

He was clearly — defiantly — not busy. The real problem seemed to be that he was out of sausage.

Ever hopeful, Karen turned right on her quest for black bread, toward the Palace Bridge, which led to Nevsky Prospekt and the center of the city. Laura turned left, walking down the University Embankment to the Builders' Bridge that led to Dormitory Number Six. She had to write a paper for Grammar class on "A Typical Day at My American University."

Leningrad State University dominated Vasilievsky Island, which sat in the middle of the Neva River like an iceberg, dividing it into the Big Neva and the Little Neva. Karen was headed over the Big Neva toward the main part of the city, where most of the major tourist attractions — Nevsky Prospekt, the Hermitage, fancy hotels, other museums and monuments — glittered in the winter sun. Laura prepared to cross the Little Neva to Petrovsky Island, where their dorm — a special dorm for foreigners — stood apart from the main university campus, keeping the foreign students and their bad Western influence safely isolated from the rest of the kids.

At the midpoint of the bridge, when it was too late to turn back, there they were: two gypsy women carrying baby-shaped bundles, their black scarves flapping like crows' wings, posted like Scylla and Charybdis to assault anyone who tried to pass. There were always at least two gypsy women on the bridge, and they always carried what looked like bundled infants. Laura had yet to see a baby's face in those bundles, or hear a cry. It struck her as strange that all the gypsy women should have babies exactly the same age, and none older than six months. Where were the gypsy toddlers?

She took a deep breath and charged forward. She had to get across the bridge somehow. It was by far the shortest way back to the dorm, and walking farther than necessary in the bitter cold was not appealing.

"*Daitye kopeiki! Daitye! Daitye!*" The women swarmed Laura, sweeping the baby bundles under her nose just fast enough so that she couldn't see inside. "Give us kopecks for the babies!"

At orientation, Laura's American professor chaperones, the husband-and-wife team of Dr. Stein (wife) and Dr. Durant (husband), had warned the students not to give money to the gypsies, for once you did, they'd never leave you alone. Laura dreaded this confrontation on the bridge every day, twice a day, and even though she suspected that there were no babies — not in those bundles, anyway — she could hardly keep herself from reaching into her pocket for a few thin brown coins. Karen had always stopped her before, but now Karen wasn't here, and Laura's resistance was low. If those babies were hungry, she knew how they felt.

She pulled off her gloves and dug into the pockets of her heavy sheepskin coat, but they were empty. She hadn't brought any money with her. "Forgive me," she said, struggling to find the Russian words under the stress of the moment. "No money. Nothing."

The women stood in front of her, blocking her passage across the bridge. Their eyes flashed angrily. By stopping, she'd raised their hopes for a handout, and now they wanted the payoff.

"You have it. Give it to us!"

Laura shook her head emphatically, hoping they'd understand. "I'm sorry. I don't." She stepped to the side, and they closed in on her.

"Please!" The English words burst out of her involuntarily. "I'll bring something next time!"

She pushed past them, not too hard for fear that those bundles might hold real babies after all, and started to run, awkward and bumbling in her bulky coat and boots, slipping on the icy surface of the bridge. The gypsy women chased her, quicker and nimbler than she was. They managed to get in front of her again, waving those swaddled bundles as if they might swat her with them, in a way that definitely suggested there weren't any babies inside.

"Give it to us!" One woman grabbed at Laura's book bag, tearing it open and reaching inside. The other stuffed her hands in Laura's pockets, pulling out a Kleenex and tossing it down in frustration.

"Let me go!" Laura shouted, again in English. She tried to pull away, but they clutched at her coat, holding her back, threatening to topple her onto the ice. Her mind frantically grappled for the right Russian words to make them go away, a magic spell to make the witches disappear.

And then, like magic, the words arrived. Not in her brain, but on the metallic air.

"Stop! Go away. Now!"

A young man ran up from the dorm side of the bridge, shooing the gypsies away as if they were pigeons. They paused for a second to stare at him, gauging how dangerous he might be. As if to answer their unspoken question, he added, "*Militsia!*" The gypsies took off, clutching the bundles to their chests, and disappeared over the arc of the bridge, back toward the university.

"Come on," the man said to Laura in heavily accented English. He took her hand and together they ran the rest of the way over the bridge, laughing as if they'd just gotten away with something.

On the other side they stopped to catch their breath.

"Thank you," she said in Russian.

He smiled and bowed his head. "It was nothing," he said, also in Russian. At her comprehending nod, he added, "You speak Russian?"

"Not perfectly. I'm studying it."

He tugged his knit cap over his wavy brown hair. On his boyish face — smooth fair skin, rosy cheeks, mischievous brown eyes — sat a short mustache. It looked out of place, almost fake, a contradiction of that tender boyishness. He couldn't have been much older than she was. Had he grown it in an attempt to look mature, or intimidating? She'd seen a lot of mustaches in Leningrad. Maybe it was a style thing — a Russian style thing that she didn't get at all.

"Stay away from the gypsies," he warned her. "They're thieves. You shouldn't give them money."

"That's what I was told."

"They're afraid of the militia. All you have to do is say the word."

"I'll remember that."

"But then, who isn't afraid of the militia?" He didn't laugh, but turned up one corner of his mouth — the mustache tilted rakishly — to show that he was joking, sort of. "Where are you from?"

"America."

His eyes lit up. Everyone's always did. The word *America* was also like a magic spell, conjuring a fantasy of cars, clothes, comfort, riches.

"What is your name, girl from America?"

"Laura Reid."

"Alexei Mikhailovich Nikolayev." He pulled her still-ungloved hand to his lips and kissed it like a count out of Tolstoy.

Laura laughed nervously. No one had ever kissed her hand before. She couldn't shake the disoriented feeling that she'd somehow landed in a weird foreign movie. "Hello, Alexei."

"Hello, Laoora. Call me Alyosha."

He wore a blue parka with a fur-trimmed hood and, unlike anyone else she'd seen in this frigid January weather, sneakers. A small duffel bag hung from one shoulder, and in his free hand he clutched something wrapped in greasy paper. He held this up to her now. Inside the paper were two small piroshki, meat pies sold by babushkas from carts on the street.

"Are you hungry?" He handed her a small meat pie, wrapped in flaky dough and still warm. "Take this."

"Thank you." She bit into it gratefully. It was savory and delicious.

They stood at the foot of the bridge, neither one sure which way to go next. Three streets fanned out in front of them, forks in a road.

"This is where I'm going," Laura said. Dormitory Number Six loomed, bulky and ugly, straight ahead. Alyosha couldn't go inside with her. A guard named Ivan was stationed in the lobby, and everyone who entered had to show his or her passport to him.

Alyosha smiled a little sadly. "Okay."

She took a step toward the dorm, one step, but something made her stop. She couldn't leave him there. Not yet. Not after he'd rescued her from the gypsies and fed her the most savory meat pie ever baked. She owed him something.

"How can I thank you?" she asked him.

He shrugged. "Take a walk with me?"

There was nothing threatening or dangerous about him, and so far all he'd done was help her. And somehow, even though the afternoon was quickly darkening, she no longer felt cold. Perhaps the meat pie had warmed her bones.

"All right," she told him.

They walked through the dreary neighborhood beyond her dorm, the streets cluttered with nondescript apartment buildings and shops. A long line formed outside Store Number 47.

Alyosha nodded at the line but showed no interest in joining it. "They must have something good for sale," he observed. "Maybe cucumbers. Or toilet paper."

Laura didn't know what to say. She hated the way she had to struggle to come up with words in Russian. She'd studied for years, since high school, and yet somehow in real conversations her mind kept going blank.

"Do you live around here?" she finally managed to ask.

"No. I live in Avtovo." She had no idea where that was, and it must have showed on her face, because he added, "Second to last stop on the metro. Far away."

"Oh." She hadn't been on the metro yet, but she'd looked at the map and knew that the city was huge, and that he must live on the outskirts. So what was he doing on Vasilievsky Island, walking around near the university?

"You are studying at the university?" he asked her.

"Yes. Until June."

He nodded. They turned a corner and passed another long line, this one for vodka. A grizzled gray man with both front teeth missing grinned and pointed at her. She ignored him.

"Your Russian is pretty good."

"Ha-ha. Thank you."

"Of course you need a little practice. That's normal."

"I take five classes at the university," Laura said. "Phonetics, Composition, Grammar, Translation, and —"

He cut her off. "Classes won't help you. You need experience. In real life. To learn the real Russian."

She nodded. It was hard to argue with that.

"And I would like to practice my English," he added.

"Say something in English," she said.

He gave a hesitant smile. "Eh . . . hello, Laura. Is nice day? I drive convertible car."

She laughed. "That's good."

"You're laughing at me." He was speaking Russian again.

"No! It's good! My Russian is no better." Though she secretly suspected it was.

"Will you help me? We could practice together." He stopped and rummaged through his duffel bag until he found a pencil and a scrap of paper. He wrote his name and a number on the paper and gave it to her. "This is my phone number. You can call me anytime."

"Okay." The numbers were neatly written, squared off like little designs.

"But listen." They were a block away from the dorm. He didn't seem to want to go farther. "Do not call me from the phone in your dorm." He pointed to a red phone booth on the corner. "And not from this phone. Or from a phone booth anywhere near the university."

"Then where should I call you from?"

He looked down the street, away from the dorm. "Walk five blocks that way — at least five blocks — and find a phone booth on the street. You can call me from there."

"All right." This was strange. Was he joking? They were no longer in a Tolstoy novel; now it was a spy story.

"Do you promise?"

"Yes. I promise. But why?"

He spoke in a low voice, almost a whisper. "Any phone booth near your dorm is sure to be bugged. They like to know what the foreign students are up to."

"Oh." They *were* in a spy novel. Or at least he thought they were. "Who are *they*?"

He flashed her a skeptical, pitying look, as if to say *You really don't know?* And she did know what he meant, sort of. She'd heard stories of rooms that were bugged, American students sent home for fraternizing with the wrong people, Russian friends getting arrested for reasons that struck Americans as arbitrary and mysterious, impossible to understand. This was a totalitarian government, after all, and the sense that the government could do anything to anyone without explanation led to rampant paranoia.

"Do you promise to call me?" he asked.

She wasn't sure, but she said, "I promise."

"Good." They stood awkwardly on the corner for a few seconds. A stocky, gray-haired woman bustled by with her string bag full of potatoes, giving Laura a good stare. "I would walk you to your dormitory, but I can't."

"I understand."

"So you go, and I'll go back over the bridge to the metro."

"All right. Thank you for the pie. And for saving me on the bridge."

"It's nothing. You'll call me?"

"I'll call."

She walked down the block to the dorm, pausing at the front door. She saw him in the distance, hiking over the bridge. He didn't look back.

She looked at his phone number again, then put it in her coat pocket. For the first time since she'd arrived, she had someone to call, and the simple act of calling him was suffused with intrigue. Leningrad seemed to glimmer subtly in the growing dusk. The city was a new world. She felt herself being drawn in.

She'd call him. She knew she would.

2

★

LENIN SPELLED BACKWARD

*L*aura Reid could trace her interest in Russian to one particular day when she was ten.

Her fifth-grade teacher had read a book to the class called *The Endless Steppe*, by Esther Hautzig. Esther was a Jewish girl living in Poland during World War II whose family was arrested by the Soviets and exiled to Siberia. They starved, worked in the mines, and struggled to survive. It was the most terrible story Laura had ever heard, and she couldn't stop thinking about it. The hardships of Siberia gripped her dreams at night as she snuggled in her warm, comfortable bed in her big, happy house in Baltimore.

She was taking French then, but her school offered Russian starting in the ninth grade. A senior came to Laura's fifth-grade class to show a film on the history of the Russian czars: an endless parade of murder, insanity, terror, and betrayal set in wintry, golden palaces. The film included pivotal scenes acted out by "ghosts" — no actors were shown, but somehow invisible hands plunged knives into chests and hurled maces onto skulls. The scene that clinched it for Laura was the one where Ivan the Terrible — the name alone gave her a delicious shiver — killed his own son. The golden staff he used to murder his child crashed down onto an oriental carpet, which was quickly stained by a pool of blood. The camera closed in on a famous painting showing Ivan, his eyes bulging in horror, cradling his son's bloody head, violins shrieking on the sound track.

That's what did it.

These people were crazy! Even Richard Nixon — the worst president in American history — would never kill one of his children.

She decided that day to study Russian, the language of violence, terror, and absurdity. She knew she would never be bored.

And someday she would go to Russia to see it all for herself.

She showed her passport and student ID to Ivan, the guard who sat in a glassed-in booth in the dormitory entrance, keeping people who didn't belong there — all Soviets except for a few carefully chosen, officially approved university students — away from the tantalizing foreigners. Ivan also guarded the one telephone in the building. Laura was only allowed to call her parents twice over the course of the semester, unless there was an emergency. She had to make an appointment weeks in advance and hope her parents were home when she called, or else she'd have to wait for the next appointment to talk to them. And the calls were outrageously expensive.

Back in the States, in college, her parents had called her every Sunday. She'd resented it, their nosy questions, their hopeful prying. She told them about her classes and her friends, leaving out details like that she was hungover from Saturday night's party, or that she was crazy about a senior named Josh, who, so far at least, didn't seem all that crazy about her.

Now that she couldn't just pick up a phone and call her parents, she missed them. She missed her college roommate, Julie, who kept telling her Josh was an asshole. And she missed Josh, who was an asshole sometimes, but other times he had a midnight magnetism, a way of making romance out of ordinary moments, that she could really use right now. They'd play heated rounds of Space Invaders in the Grad Center Bar, share a pitcher of beer and some kisses at the jukebox, arguing over whether to play the Clash or Rick James. They might end up in his off-campus apartment, stretched out on the ratty couch in the candlelight with a streetlamp shining in through the window, sharing a joint. That was when Josh would start to drift away from her, and she'd feel an ache she didn't understand. But she missed even that, the drift and the ache.

She walked up the dingy dorm stairwell, beige walls smudged and peeling, to the third floor, where the Americans and the Hungarians lived with their Soviet roommates. The halls were lit with long strips of fluorescent lights, bright and depressing, and the linoleum was littered with chicken bones, cockroach casings, and gray balls of dust.

Donovan Platt rolled by, tipping his cowboy hat to her, his long black hair in a ponytail. "Afternoon, ma'am," he drawled. He was on his way out to conduct his mysterious business, tall and lanky in blue jeans, jean jacket, down vest, cowboy hat, and cowboy boots.

"Where are you off to?" Laura asked idly, just to see how he'd answer. Theoretically the American students were supposed to speak Russian to one another all the time, but none of them did. After a long day of grappling with dense Russian consonants, the slangy ease of English rushed out of her, a glorious relief.

"I've got some people to see, business to attend to."

"All right, then." Donovan had arrived in September with a small group of American students who'd planned to study in Leningrad for a whole year. By the time Laura's group had arrived in January, half of them were gone, unable to stand the conditions any longer. The ones who'd stayed had gone crazy. Donovan didn't bother with classes anymore. He was dealing on the black market — currency, jeans, even drugs, Laura had heard — making tons of money. If caught, he could end up in a Soviet prison that made American jails look like Club Med. For ordinary Soviets, having foreign money in their possession automatically meant prison. Planting Western currency on an unsuspecting citizen was a time-honored way to frame someone. The authorities dealt with the Westerners who provided the money on a case-by-case basis, but everyone knew it was a serious offense. Donovan didn't seem to care.

Lydia Macy, another year-long student hanging on by her fingernails, shuffled by in a flannel nightgown and fuzzy blue slippers, her hair stringy and limp. "Hey, Lydia," Laura said.

"Hey." Lydia ducked into the kitchen and put a pot of water on the stove for tea. She was bony and wild-eyed. She never left the dorm, never even got dressed. She looked anorexic, but Donovan said the real problem was she'd drunk the tap water without boiling it. Now she had a parasite in her gut that she refused to treat.

"Are you going to the Hungarians' party later?" Laura asked.

"They didn't invite me." Lydia sat down on a rickety chair and picked at a sticky clump of fuzz on her slipper.

"I'm sure Ilona would invite you if she saw you. It's Barto's birthday."

The kettle boiled. "I hate birthday parties." Lydia poured water into her mug. "What's up with your roommate, anyway?"

"Which one?" Laura lived with Karen and Ninel, a Spanish major from the Ukraine.

"The bitchy one. I was feeding sardines to a couple of the cats and she came out and yelled at me for wasting good food on strays."

"That's Ninel. She's weird," Laura said. "She likes to follow the rules." The dorm was riddled with rules: a ten o'clock curfew, no guests allowed, no spending the night outside the dorm, no loud music . . .

"So do most of the clones they put in this dorm, but she's more robotic than any of them."

"She probably wanted to eat the sardines herself." Tins of sardines were hard to come by, unless you were a foreigner who could shop at the special stores. To Ninel they would have been a treat.

"If I want to give my sardines to some cats, what business is it of hers?"

"Why don't you come to the party tonight?" Laura said. "At least get dressed. It might make you feel better."

"I feel fine." She sipped her tea and crossed her legs one over the other, swinging the top leg up and down like a scissors blade.

"*Chiquitas*." Maureen Binkowski, known as Binky, duck-walked in and looked around in bewilderment, as if she expected to find a refrigerator in the kitchen, even though she knew better. "I would murder for a Tab right now. I always have a Tab and a Ring Ding every day at four o'clock. This is killing me. I don't know how I'm going to make it through the evening."

"Have some tea," Lydia suggested.

"I'm so sick of tea I could puke." Binky looked like she'd just arrived by spaceship. She was tiny, with large pink glasses and a poofy fro of yellow hair. She wore a bright orange down coat and blue-and-silver moon boots everywhere she went. "In fact, if I did puke, it would be nothing but tea."

"You miss Tab? Just wait." Lydia began to laugh, quietly at first, then louder and kind of like a maniac. Binky looked at

Laura over Lydia's shaking head, her eyes wide behind her over-sized old-lady glasses.

The Americans loved to complain about all the things they missed from home, but they had come to this land of deprivation voluntarily. Most of them were required to spend some time in the USSR as Russian Studies majors. None of them had realized how hard it would be to go without the comforts they took for granted.

"Yeah. I'll see you at the party." Binky hurried out, and Laura followed. She could still hear Lydia cackling as she walked down the hall and went into the triple room she shared with Karen and Ninel. Ninel sat at the round table in the center, studying Spanish grammar. Laura plopped down on her narrow metal bed. "*Prívyet*, Nina." Everyone called her Nina for short, which was a relief, since Ninel was such a strange name. Laura didn't notice until Karen pointed it out to her: *Nínel* was *Lenín* spelled backward.

Nina had an older sister named Elektrifikatsia and a brother named Traktor. She kept a photo of her family on her night-stand. They posed, stiff and formal, in a photographer's studio, against a backdrop of waving wheat.

"Good evening, Laura." Laura and Karen always spoke Russian with Nina because she didn't speak English. "What did you learn in school today?"

"Hmm." Laura tried to remember what she'd learned in her Russian classes that day. "In Phonetics we learned how to sing 'Moscow Nights,' and in Grammar we read an article about how washers and dryers are plentiful throughout the Soviet Union."

"Interesting." Nina nodded as if she really found that interesting.

Nina had grown up outside Kiev. She was studying Spanish and wanted to be a Spanish teacher in Siberia, where, she said, it was nice and quiet. She made it sound like there'd be lots of chances to speak Spanish in Siberia. Maybe she even believed it.

Laura sat on her bed and started her homework. This is what she wrote (translated into English):

A Typical Day at My American University

I go to Brown University in Providence, Rhode Island. On a typical day I get up around ten o'clock, in time for Comparative Literature class, which starts at eleven o'clock. I don't choose classes that start early because I don't like to get up in the morning. After "Comp Lit," as we call it for short, I go to the Blue Room to get coffee and listen in on my fellow students. They talk about urgent issues like how much money their parents spent on their little sisters' sweet sixteen parties, or which expensive private school has the best lacrosse team. As you can see, American life is very decadent. But then, you already knew that.

After lunch, if I feel like it, I go to my Russian Literature class, followed by a class known as Clapping for Credit, where all we do is watch movies. Then I might meet my boyfriend, Josh, at the Grad Center Bar for a beer and waste a few hours playing video games. I return to my dorm at eleven or so and read for a couple of hours before passing out on my bed still wearing my clothes.

And that's a typical day at my American university. The end.

Laura read over the essay, correcting grammar mistakes. What she'd written was true and not true. She thought about the things she didn't mention, the spaces between the lines where her real life happened.

Like, if she ran into Josh at lunch, she might not make it to her afternoon classes. He might lure her to the Grad Center Bar for just one game of Space Invaders, which would lead to another and another, and maybe a pitcher of beer, until it was dark outside and they'd missed dinner. So they'd order a pizza and go back to his off-campus apartment. If his roommates were out, they'd veg in front of the TV until Josh started pawing her. They'd end up in his room, and she'd spend the night. In the morning, he'd make her a cup of coffee and send her on her way, even if she didn't have any morning classes. He always said he had a lot to do that day.

If his pretty roommate, Alison, was home, Josh would sit on the couch and talk to her and they'd trade inside jokes and basically ignore Laura until eleven or so, when Laura would start wondering if Josh wanted her to stay over or not. If he was still flirting with Alison at midnight, Laura would give up and go home, and Josh wouldn't seem to mind. In fact, she got the feeling he was relieved. She'd walk home through the quiet, tree-lined streets of College Hill feeling confused and lonely. Back at Laura's dorm, her suitemate giggling with her boyfriend behind her closed door, she'd put the radio on "Jazz After Hours," and read until she fell asleep.

Still, she missed it. Having a room all to herself. Doing whatever she pleased. No rigorous schedule full of classes and field trips. Potable tap water. Pizza. Jazz on the radio. Josh.

Karen came in with a box of soft cookies and a couple of bottles of fizzy water.

"You remembered mineral water — thank God," Laura said.

"You can actually *taste* the minerals!" Karen joked. The water did have a strong metallic taste.

"Yes, thanks to God that you don't have to drink the same water everyone else drinks," Nina said. "The sacred water that saved millions of lives during the Great Patriotic War."

Nina was great with the conversation stoppers. Laura hardly dared to look at Karen for fear they'd both burst out laughing. Not that World War II was funny . . .

Laura grabbed her toothbrush and reached for a bottle of mineral water. "Like I said, thank God." Then off to the sink room to brush her teeth.

When she came back to change for the party, she found Alyosha's number in the pocket of her cords. She looked at the neat, strangely blocky letters and felt a little gush of happiness at the memory of how he'd rescued her that afternoon. Finally, something interesting had happened.

She looked around for a safe place to hide the paper. In the end, she decided her pocket was the safest spot.

3
★
RUSSIAN TELEPHONE ETIQUETTE

*I*n Laura's Literature class the next day, they read a Pushkin poem, "To a Foreign Lady." Her classmates were her fellow Americans: Karen, Binky, Dan, and a few of the other undergrad language students. By college, a Russian student would know most of Pushkin's work by heart. Laura was reminded of Alyosha when she read the lines, "In language you won't comprehend, I write this verse to say good-bye . . ."

Not that she needed a reminder.

Don't call him today, she warned herself. *It's too soon. Wait until next week.*

But she felt restless, and she didn't trust herself to heed her own advice. Here she was in a foreign country, sitting in class with a bunch of other Americans, just like she would be at home. Reading about love.

Pathetic, that's what it was. Timid. Boring. She was wasting her youth — her "fleeting youth," as Pushkin might have said.

Fleeting. No time to waste.

She longed for something to happen to her. Something exciting. It was up to her to make it happen, to take chances. Take action.

If she couldn't find an adventure in Russia, she deserved to be bored.

When classes ended for the day, she left the university without stopping for lunch. She bypassed the pay phone in the hall, bypassed the phone booth outside the cafeteria. Karen caught up with her at the OGNEOPASNO! sign and asked, "Where are you off to in such a hurry?"

"No hurry. I'm just restless."

"I know what you mean; I can't get out of class fast enough."

Laura wanted to tell Karen about Alyosha. She ached to tell someone. But it was better to wait. She'd only known Karen a couple of weeks. What if she called Alyosha and he didn't remember her? What if they planned to meet and he stood her up? There were so many ways this situation could turn out to be humiliating. The fewer people to witness it, the better.

She was glad to have Karen's company for the trek over the Builders' Bridge, though. The gypsies didn't bother them now. They cowered on the other side of the bridge, their long scarves flapping in the wind, and did not approach.

"What's up with the gypsies?" Karen asked. "I've been practicing my brush-off. Look." Karen walked briskly forward, swinging her arms and keeping her eyes straight ahead, muttering, "No, no, no, sorry, no."

Laura laughed. "Impressive."

"Right? So now they're not going to give me a chance to brush them off? How diabolically clever." Karen dared to glance back at the coterie. "They look almost . . . spooked."

"Weird," Laura said. She smiled to herself. They were afraid of her now.

Russian gypsies afraid of *her*.

On the other side of the river, Karen turned toward the dorm as usual, but Laura paused.

Walk five blocks past the dorm, she thought, remembering his instructions. *At least five blocks . . .*

"Home sweet home," Karen said. "Aren't you coming?"

Maybe she shouldn't call him. What was with the secrecy? Who was he, really?

"Hello? Laura? It's freezing out. . . ."

Maybe he was a womanizer, racking up notches on his bedpost. Maybe he was a spy. A double agent! Or just a jerk.

She shouldn't call him. But she would anyway.

"I'm going to go for a walk," Laura said.

"A walk?" Karen pulled her scarf over her nose and shivered. "In this weather?" It was getting dim, and the moisture in the air sparkled and bit at their exposed skin. "You're either part polar bear or you're crazy." She hurried inside without waiting for an answer from Laura about her possible ursine parentage or mental illness.

"I'm crazy!" Laura shouted after her, but Karen disappeared inside without looking back, the heavy brown door slamming shut behind her.

Laura walked down the street, away from the river, glancing around to see if anyone was following her. People gaped at her in her sheepskin coat, but no one seemed to be trailing her.

She passed a line of men waiting for kvass to be dispensed like oil from a tanker truck. She passed a busy bakery and a tobacco shop. She walked five blocks, then one more for good measure, until she found a red phone booth. She looked around once more for spies, but the coast was clear. She pulled Alyosha's number from her coat pocket, slotted a two-kopeck coin into the phone, and dialed before she had a chance to change her mind.

"*Allo?*"

"*Allo.* Is this Alyosha?" Laura asked in Russian. It felt strange to speak Russian over the phone. She had to concentrate to remember the words.

"Is this Laura?"

Her accent must have given her away. "It's Laura. How are you?"

"I'm very well. And you?"

It was just like a practice conversation in class. "I'm fine, thank you."

A silence followed. She thought he'd know why she was calling, but if he did, he didn't say so.

"Um, so, I'm calling to see if you would like to meet with me sometime. To practice speaking Russian. As you can hear, I need practice badly."

"Not so badly. Yes, let's meet. When are you free?"

"Every afternoon after three."

"Okay, how about Tuesday, then?"

"Tuesday is good." *Four days away, though.*

"Do you know Dom Knigi?" Everyone knew Dom Knigi, the House of Books. It was the biggest bookstore in Leningrad, a nineteenth-century landmark on Nevsky Prospekt topped with a bronze-and-glass globe. "Meet me in the poetry section at three thirty."

"All right." She paused, waiting for him to say something more. She tried to remember what he looked like but could only see his brown eyes. A long stretch of seconds passed in silence. At last he said, "I'm glad you called, Laura. See you then."

"Good-bye." She hung up the phone and stood in the narrow red booth, staring through the glass at a stray dog skulking down the street, hugging the wall of a building, tongue hanging out.

Her heart was racing, and she wasn't sure why. They were just meeting for coffee, meeting for language practice. What was so adventurous about that?

She left the phone booth and, checking once more for spies and finding none, started back for the dorm. On the way, she stopped to buy a loaf of bread and a bag of strange, hard little mini-bagels. She wondered what kvass tasted like — it was made of fermented bread — but there were no women in the line, only men; grizzled, wino-type men. If she joined the line, it would surely cause some kind of stir. Maybe someday Alyosha would get some for her to taste. Someday, if they became friends.

4

★

MEETING AT THE HOUSE OF BOOKS

*O*n Tuesday afternoon, Laura crossed the Palace Bridge over the Big Neva River, passed the Hermitage with its parking lot full of tourist buses, and made her way down Nevsky Prospekt. She'd dressed with extra care that morning, although the weather was so cold there wasn't much choice — she pretty much had to wear corduroys, a turtleneck, boots, and a warm sweater under her coat. But she made sure to pick the black turtleneck that had no holes under the arms, and her favorite blue sweater with the buttons at the neck.

The streets bustled with shoppers, mostly women in bulky coats and children leaving school, the girls' hair braided and tied with oversized white bows. She passed the Aeroflot office, glamorous in a sleek, space-age, 1960s-stewardess way, like the Pan Am building in New York. She crossed intricate iron bridges over winding canals, thinking about Fyodor Dostoyevsky, who once paced these very streets, tortured by thoughts of good and evil, holiness and sin.

The giant globe on top of Dom Knigi gleamed, a beacon over the Griboyedov Canal. The bookstore ruled its corner of Nevsky Prospekt like an Art Nouveau duchess, guarded by a bronze eagle and crowned with a glass-and-bronze tower that lit up at night. Two bronze nymphs hoisted a globe on top of the tower like a cherry. Laura pushed through the door and wandered the aisles of books until she found the poetry section. Alyosha leaned against a shelf, absorbed in a volume of Vladimir Mayakovsky: *A Cloud in Trousers*.

He sensed her, though. When she appeared, he looked up from his book with genuine pleasure — pleased to see her, pleased with life.

"You came!" he whispered in Russian. "I wasn't sure." He leaned forward and kissed her on both cheeks. "*Zdravstvuitye*, Laura."

"*Zdravstvuitye*." The kiss startled her. His cheek was smooth but the mustache tickled. "What are you reading?"

He chose a line from the open book. "'If you wish, I shall grow irreproachably tender: not a man, but a cloud in trousers!'"

She laughed at the image of a man so transformed by love that he became as delicate and wispy as a cloud.

"Want some coffee? Let's go." He replaced the book and led her outside. They walked up the street to a busy café. She followed him to the cashier, where he paid for two coffees and a roll and took the receipt to a steamy counter where women in stained white aprons sloshed milky coffee out of large vats and into glasses.

There were no tables, so they took their coffees to a counter by the fogged-up window. He set the roll in front of her. "For you."

"Thank you." The roll was warm and sweet.

"How do you like our beautiful city?"

"It's very cold," Laura said. "But it is beautiful. Like a big frozen cake." She decided not to mention how grimy and depressing she found it. That would be rude.

"Maybe I could take you on a tour. You've been to the Hermitage by now, I guess?"

She nodded. "But I plan to go again, lots of times. I love the Leonardos."

"And have you been to the Russian Museum?"

"The icons. Yes."

"St. Isaac's Cathedral?"

"Very impressive."

"The Fortress of Peter and Paul?"

"Yes."

"Here's one place I think you haven't been: the Museum of Hygiene. Have you been to the Museum of Hygiene?"

She laughed. "No."

"They have a wonderful exhibit on the physical consequences of bad habits like smoking," he said. "Disgusting! And they have Pavlov's dog — the original! Stuffed."

"I'd like to see that."

"I don't know. . . . The anatomy displays might be too gruesome for you. Next time we meet, I'll take you to the Museum of Religion and Atheism."

"Um, okay." She shifted her weight from one foot to the other. Why was he acting so stiff and tour-guidey? This wasn't what she wanted at all. She got enough of that cultural-exchange stuff at the university. Everyone she met hid behind an official happy face: *See our historical wonders, let's have a cultural exchange, the youth of the world must find common ground, blah blah blah . . .*

The café was steamy. She unbuttoned her coat. She didn't really know anything about this boy, so she decided to start with the basics — which suited her vocabulary.

"Are you a student?" she asked.

"No, I'm an artist. A painter."

"Oh." The blunt tips of his long fingers tapped the glass of coffee — they looked like an artist's hands. One nail was smudged with a chip of bright blue. Under his coat he wore a V-neck sweater and an orange T-shirt.

"I paint signs for movie theaters. The names of the movies, the times they are playing, maybe a scene from a film. That's my job. Very boring."

"It doesn't sound too bad. You should try working at McDonald's."

"McDonald's?"

"It's a restaurant." She tried to translate *fast food* and *chain* into Russian but he looked blank. "They sell hamburgers."

"It's good to work in a restaurant," he said. "You have access to all that food."

"Um . . . yeah." She wondered if anyone ever took a job at McDonald's because they wanted to eat more of it.

They sipped their coffees and watched the fur hats bob past the steamy glass window. The silence grew, a barrier between them. Finally, Laura said, "We are supposed to be practicing speaking, but we are not saying much."

"I'm sorry," he said. "I'm not good at this. All I can think of are the English dialogues we learned in school." He switched into stilted English: " 'Good afternoon. My name is Mr. Smith. I would like to buy a train ticket to Boston City, please.' 'Yes, Mr. Smith. One-way ticket to Boston City. Pay me two dollars, please.' "

Laura laughed. "Boston City! Where's that?"

"In the Republic of New England, of course. Don't you know your American geography?" He didn't smile, but his eyes sparkled just a little, so that she couldn't tell if he was teasing her or not.

"Why don't you teach me some Russian vocabulary?" she

suggested. "For example . . . what's that?" She pointed to her glass.

"*Shchenok*," Alyosha said.

She squinted skeptically at him. She was pretty sure he'd just said *puppy*, not *glass* or *coffee* or anything close.

"Okay . . . what's this?" She held up her glove.

"Flower," he replied in Russian.

"It's not a flower," she said.

"Which one of us is the native speaker here?" he asked.

"You are, but —"

"It's an idiom," he insisted.

"If you say so." She pointed to her right eye, which she was absolutely sure she knew the word for. "What do you call this?"

"A star," he said.

"Now I know you're teasing me," she said. "It's my eye."

"To you it may be just an eye. To me it is a beam of light from galaxies away."

She stared at him, taken aback. She didn't know whether to feel flattered or foolish. "Is that from a poem?"

He only smiled mysteriously. Then he looked at their empty glasses and asked, "Want to take a walk?"

They left the café and pressed up along Nevsky against a stiff wind. Alyosha pointed out landmarks: the Museum of Religion and Atheism, the Stroganov Palace, the Barricade Cinema, the Moika Canal, the yellow Admiralty building with its pointed golden spire. They passed an old school where flowers had been laid at the gate. Painted on the wall was a pale blue rectangle with the Russian words for *Citizens! In the event of artillery fire, this side of the street is the most DANGEROUS!* Next to that was a marble plaque: *This notice has been preserved to commemorate the heroism and courage of Leningrad's citizens during the 900-day blockade of 1941–1943.*

"The Great Patriotic War," Alyosha said. "To the rest of the world, it ended forty years ago, but here we still live with it every day."

Laura knew that over twenty million Soviet people died during World War II, and as many as two million died — from disease, hunger, or bombs — during the German siege of Leningrad. "I can feel it. The sadness, I mean. All over the city."

"Of course you can. Russians hate to let go of suffering. They will hang on to it forever if they can."

He scowled, and she knew he was angry about something, but she wasn't sure what. She had a feeling they weren't talking about World War II anymore.

That was okay with her. What she really wanted to talk about was the day. The walk. The two of them.

It was dark out now, and the wind off the river chafed their faces. Alyosha stopped for a moment to look at her. She waited for him to say something, but he didn't. Her eyes watered from the cold. He lifted her woolen scarf and pulled it up over her chin to warm her.

"Thank you," she said.

He smiled a wry, off-center grin that held a hint of sadness in its playfulness. Something twinged inside her, like the snapping of a wishbone.

They walked a little farther until they reached the Palace Bridge. Had something happened between them just then? She felt it, but couldn't articulate it, even in her own mind. Every few steps she stole a glance at his face. She could swear she saw him wrestling with the same questions in his mind.

Or maybe she imagined it. Probably. That would be like her.

At the bridge, he said, "I'll leave you here."

"You go your way and I'll go mine," Laura replied, keeping her tone light.

He took both her gloved hands in his and kissed her stinging cheeks. "Will you call me again?"

"Yes." *Yes, yes, for sure, yes.*

"Good-bye."

She crossed the bridge, while he turned back and walked down Nevsky to the metro, his head ducked against the sharp wind.

5

★

BREAKING THE RULES

*B*inky Binkowsky, the yellow-haired girl with the moon boots, had mentioned something about a five-day rule. First, she said, you should never call a guy, but always wait for him to call. But Alyosha couldn't call the dorm, so Laura asked, "What if you have to call him for some reason?"

"Then wait at least five days from the last time you talked to him or saw him," Binky pronounced. "Unless it's an emergency."

"Let me ask you something, Binky," Karen said. "How many guys have you dated?"

"Not very many." She pressed on her oversized pink glasses. "Okay, none. But when I find the right guy, I will know exactly how to handle him."

Karen nodded, but later she said to Laura, "I wouldn't take love advice from a person named Binky."

There was another reason to be cautious. The Americans had been warned during orientation, before they'd even arrived in Leningrad, to beware of falling in love. For most Russians, there was only one way to leave the Soviet Union, and that was to marry a foreigner. Some of them would do anything, say anything, to get to the West, especially America. "Be on guard!" her chaperones had told them. "Don't fall for it."

Nevertheless, two days after her first coffee with Alyosha, Laura found her feet moving down the street by themselves toward the faraway phone booth, a two-kopek coin burning in her hand. The paper with his number on it was smudged, as if she'd worn out the ink just by looking at it too much.

She dialed the number. No answer.

Laura cursed the Soviets and their lack of answering machines.

She waited a few minutes. Maybe he was in the shower. Maybe he was just about to walk in the door. She stepped outside the phone booth and looked around. The street was quiet, but a man in a fur hat and black-rimmed glasses loitered on the corner. Was he watching her? No, he had a dog with him, on a leash. Just out walking his dog. Probably. Unless it was a front. Dog-walking would be the perfect spy front. Maybe she should try another phone booth.

She crossed the street and walked even farther from the dorm. Two blocks later she found another phone booth. She glanced back. No sign of the man with the glasses.

She stepped inside and dialed Alyosha again. Still no answer. She'd just have to wait another day.

Maybe this is a good thing, she told herself. *Maybe the universe is protecting me from my own worst instincts. If Binky's right, I'll seem overeager.*

No. There was no way Binky could be right.

I'll just try him one more time. One more time. Then I'll go back and do my Translation homework.

She slipped the coin into the slot and dialed. *Ring . . . ring . . . ring . . .* "*Allo?*"

She was so startled she couldn't speak for a second. The words caught in her throat.

"*Allo?*"

"Alyosha? It's me, Laura."

"Laura! I'm so happy you called. I was just thinking about you. I went to the market and they had some very pretty blue flowers — Imagine! A miracle! — and they made me think of you. So I bought them, thinking, Laura would like these, even though I have no idea if you even like flowers —"

"— I do —"

"Of course you do! Who doesn't like flowers? I'm going to put them on my kitchen table. They're for you, even if you never see them."

"Thank you."

"When can I see you again?"

Her heart was pounding. She wasn't sure why. She just knew that she couldn't wait to see him again. "Tomorrow?"

"Yes. Perfect. I'll meet you in the same place in Dom Knigi."

"Three o'clock."

"See you then. Good-bye, Laura."

"Good-bye."

She hung up the phone and stood in the protective cocoon of the booth for a few minutes, trying to catch her breath. His voice, those Russian words, the way he pronounced her name — *Laoora, oo, oo* — did something strange to her.

She emerged from the booth. The man with the glasses and the dog turned the corner. He didn't follow her.

She went back to the dorm, taking the same streets she'd walked on the way to the phone booth. But somehow those very streets looked different now, as if they were part of a movie set and the director had changed the lighting. The piles of snow, which had been dirty and dingy before, now glittered like sequins. The cranky citizens trudging from chore to chore had transformed into jolly shoppers on their way to warm homes to make dinner. The mangy stray cats skittering down an alley became gleaming, graceful wild animals in an urban jungle. Laura whistled a song, "Only Love Can Break Your Heart," without giving much thought to the meaning of the words.

The next day, after Phonetics class, with Pushkin's words still rolling around in her mouth ("*I loved you once, in silence and despair . . .*"), Laura hurried away from the university toward the

Palace Bridge. She crossed the river and walked down Nevsky Prospekt, the globe atop Dom Knigi fixed in her sights. She tried to imagine Josh saying — or thinking — or even reading aloud — lovely words like Pushkin's. *I loved you, though, with love so deep and rare . . .* There was no way. He couldn't say something that pure without an ironic smirk, without making fun of it. Maybe no one could, anymore. After all, Aleksandr Pushkin wrote that poem in the 1820s. People were different then. Love was different then. Maybe it meant more.

Even that sad thought couldn't weigh her down, because she was on her way to a tryst. A secret, possibly dangerous, romantic meeting. That's what she told herself, whether it was true or not. She thought of Alyosha's fine, boyish face and the incongruous brushy mustache pasted on it like a costume for a school play, and smiled. A spy meeting, that's what it was. Two spies from different worlds, comparing notes, working to undermine the authorities . . .

She pushed through the doors of the bookstore and wove her way to the poetry section. Alyosha grinned at her. But something was wrong. Something was missing.

The mustache!

"I shaved it off. What do you think?"

He offered his bare upper lip for her inspection. She could see the bones of his face better. He looked younger, even younger than he was, but definitely more handsome.

"I like it."

"Good." He kissed her cheeks again, then took her hand. Her face flushed with surprise. "Let's get out of here." He led her out of the store and to Brodsky Street, where a neon sign blinked *Sadko.* "Today's lesson: speaking about food."

He gripped her gloved hand in his ungloved one. She longed to pull off her glove, in spite of the cold, and let him hold her bare hand.

He led her inside the restaurant to a large room lit by red crystal chandeliers, the high-vaulted ceilings decorated with painted-on flower garlands, the tall windows curtained with heavy red drapes. The patrons, well-groomed and expensively dressed in business suits and silky dresses, murmured in Russian, French, and German. The parquet pattern in the wooden floor was cracked in places. Laura smelled onions and browning butter.

"Have you been here before?" Alyosha asked.

"No. But it looks a lot like the dining room in the Astoria Hotel." The Astoria also had high ceilings, gold-trimmed walls, and gleaming chandeliers, though when you looked closely the walls needed painting, the linens were worn, and the chairs a bit shabby.

"My father used to bring me and my mother here on special occasions."

Interesting. Not just anyone could get a table at a fancy Nevsky Prospekt restaurant. Laura had heard that if you weren't a foreigner, a celebrity, or a Party big shot, they'd tell you the place was booked, while you stared at a roomful of empty tables.

So who was Alyosha's father?

A man in a tuxedo, his dark hair slicked down, greeted them. He looked them up and down — Laura hadn't dressed for a fancy restaurant, and neither had Alyosha — and asked how he could help them.

"I'm an Intourist guide," Alyosha explained. "And this is an American tourist."

Laura caught on right away. "Hello," she said in English.

The host gave her a once-over again, his eyes settling on her dark blue corduroys and unfamiliar boots.

"Follow me." He led them to a table beside a stained-glass window and left them with two menus. Laura opened hers and gasped.

"Look at all these dishes they have! Chicken Kiev! Beef Stroganoff!" Sadko also offered less familiar dishes like Cold Boiled Beef in Jelly and Herring with Boiled Potatoes. Laura had seen some of these dishes on the menu at the Russian Tea Room in New York, but since she'd arrived in Leningrad she'd only eaten in cafés where the menu featured Russian vinaigrette salad (potatoes, beets, and sauerkraut), meat and cabbage pies, and *shchi*, or cabbage soup. There seemed to be no shortage of cabbage. Alyosha nodded. A waiter arrived and Alyosha ordered a bottle of champagne.

"What are you going to have?" Laura asked.

"I'm going to ask for the stroganoff and go from there."

She wasn't sure what that meant. "I have to try chicken Kiev. That's the one where you cut into the chicken breast and butter squirts out?"

The champagne arrived. The bottle had a generic label that said *Soviet Champagne*. The waiter opened it with a flourish and poured them each a glass.

"To your health." Alyosha clinked her glass.

"To your health." She took a sip. A little sweet, but the bubbles were pleasantly tickly.

"May I take your order?" The waiter stood in front of them with a white napkin draped over one forearm. This restaurant was like something out of an old movie, so formal and stiff.

"Do you have the beef stroganoff?" Alyosha asked.

"No. We're out of that."

"What about the chicken Kiev?"

"Sorry, we don't have that today."

"That's a shame," Laura said. The waiter gave her a strange glare.

"Hmm . . ." Alyosha scanned the menu. "Do you have any chicken dishes at all?"

"No. No chicken."

"Beef?"

The waiter shook his head.

"Fish?"

"We have pickled herring with cream sauce."

"Ew." Laura made a face. The waiter's glare intensified. "What else do you have?"

"Potato salad, borscht, and cabbage soup."

"And that's all?"

"Who are you to complain?" the waiter snapped. "That should be enough for anyone."

"Okay, okay. Bring us some borscht." Alyosha closed the menu. The waiter stalked away.

"That's disappointing," Laura said.

"It's always this way," Alyosha said. "If they get anything good, the waiters take it for themselves."

"At least they have this lousy champagne." Laura took a sip. "Which I like anyway."

Alyosha raised his glass. "How do you toast in America?"

"Cheers," Laura replied in English.

"Cheers."

The tables around them emptied. Lunchtime was over. The waiter returned and set two bowls of lukewarm borscht in front of them. The huge room was hushed. The chandeliers seemed to be listening in.

"Why did you do it?" Laura asked.

"Do what?"

"Shave off your mustache."

"I don't know. A voice inside my head told me to do it." He crossed his eyes to indicate insanity.

She laughed. "No, really."

He put down his spoon. It clanked loudly against the china bowl. He looked at Laura's face with an almost quizzical expression, as if he might find the answer to a question there. "I had a reason, which I won't tell you yet."

"Oh."

"Anyway, a mustache always grows back."

"That's true." *What could the reason be?*   .

"I thought it might make me look . . . more American." He concentrated on his soup now. "Like the Great Gatsby."

Laura nearly spit magenta soup across the table. "What?"

"I have an American book, *The Great Gatsby*, by F. Scott Fitzgerald," Alyosha explained. "It's in English, and it has the face of a very handsome man on the cover. He's blond, with a square jaw and a straight nose and no mustache or beard. He looks so American. He's the ideal American man, I think."

"Is it a photograph?" Laura wondered if he was thinking of Robert Redford, who'd played Gatsby in the movie. He looked nothing like Alyosha, with or without facial hair.

"Yes. At first I thought it was a photograph of Fitzgerald, but someone explained that it's actually an American movie star."

"Robert Redford."

"Do you think he's handsome?"

"Sure. He's not my favorite, though."

"Who is your favorite?"

Laura had to think about it a minute. "Al Pacino."

"Al Pacino? What does he look like?"

"He looks a little bit like you. Only darker, and with a bigger nose."

"Does he have a mustache?"

"Not right now."

"Then I will go without one, too. For you."

For her! So Continental and un-American. So romantic. The idea of a boy doing something just for her was so unfamiliar she couldn't quite relax. "Don't do it for me. Don't do anything for me."

"Why not? I can't think of a better reason to do anything." He ducked his head and went back to his soup.

She took a minute to let a fizzy feeling dissolve like champagne into her bloodstream. This boy was very charming.

"Did you like the book? *The Great Gatsby?*" she asked.

"Yes, what I read of it. I can't read very fast in English. I have to stop and look up a lot of words in the dictionary, and some of the words aren't in there."

"I have the same problem in Russian. Maybe you could read the Russian translation."

"That is very hard to find." He tapped his spoon against the bowl.

"I'm pretty sure I saw one last week," Laura said. "At the Berioska Shop."

Alyosha shrugged. "I'll bet you see a lot of things at the Berioska Shop."

Laura felt a twinge of guilt. The Berioska was a special store for foreigners only. Along with a range of tourist souvenirs, it was stocked with luxuries that ordinary Russians could hardly imagine: the best caviar, furs, wines, meats, amber jewelry, hard-to-find books and music, fancy lacquered boxes. They didn't accept rubles, only US dollars, German marks, French francs, British pounds, and so on. The windows were shaded and the door guarded to keep ordinary Soviet citizens out. The government didn't want them to see the luxuries they were deprived of — but everyone knew about them anyway.

"Have you ever been inside one?" Laura asked.

"No, of course not. How could I? They check your passport."

"They've never checked my passport."

"That's because you're obviously American."

"Well . . . what if you were obviously American?"

He lifted his eyes from his bowl. "What do you mean?"

"What if I borrowed some clothes from one of my friends and we dressed you up as an American guy? I could teach you a few English phrases to say in case anyone talked to you, and maybe we could sneak you into the Berioska." Dan Knowles was just about Alyosha's size, she thought.

He grinned, then shook his head. "No. It's too dangerous."

"Dangerous? How?"

"We'll get caught, and we'll both be in trouble. You could get sent home. And I'm not ready for you to leave yet." Laura's

American chaperones, Dr. Stein and Dr. Durant, were always warning the students about infractions — from missing curfew to associating with the wrong people — that could get them sent home. But how did Alyosha know about that?

"What about you?" she asked. "What would happen to you?"

"To me? It's hard to say. I've had friends who have been arrested for less."

"Arrested!"

"I had a friend in art school who sold fur hats to foreigners on the black market. He made a lot of money until he got caught. The militia arrested him and when we saw him a few weeks later he was a different person. Very skinny, quiet. Broken. He was kicked out of school, of course."

"This isn't worth getting arrested over," Laura said. "But how would we get caught? We're just shopping. If you stay quiet, no one will know."

"They'll know," Alyosha said. "Somehow they'll know."

His mood had turned quickly from puckish to grim. She wanted to call back that mischievous spirit.

"Don't you want to see a Berioska Shop for yourself?" she asked.

"I have to admit I'm curious."

"Then let's do it."

He hesitated.

"Come on. It will be an adventure."

He lifted his glass and clinked it against hers again. "To adventure," he said. "Our next adventure together."

6

★

ADVENTURES IN BERIOSKA SHOPPING

*Y*ou're going to do what?"

Karen was having trouble understanding the plan. Maybe it was too ridiculous to be understood.

"I'm going to dress Alyosha in American clothes from head to toe and bring him into the Berioska Shop with me. What size sneakers do you think Dan wears?"

"And what are you going to do when he opens his mouth and says, 'Khallo, please to show me some rrrecords'?"

"His accent's not that bad. And anyway, I'll do all the talking."

Karen shook her head. "You are going to get into so much trouble."

"No I'm not. Besides, it's a good deed. He's never been inside a Berioska! He's very curious about it."

"Sure, they all are. That's why you're going to get walloped."

Laura knocked on Dan's door and explained her plan. Dan blinked at her, owlish behind his round, wire-rimmed glasses.

"I love this," Dan said. "I'll give you whatever you need."

She borrowed socks, shoes, a shirt, a pair of jeans, and a jacket. She considered borrowing underwear, just for pure authenticity, but Dan assured her they wouldn't be checking Alyosha that thoroughly.

"You're going to get into major trouble for this," he said. "You know that, right?"

She refused to believe it or care.

On the day of the Big Adventure, her classes felt endless. In Phonetics, Laura's favorite class, they were learning jokes.

"Our Physics teacher talks to himself. Does yours?"

"Ours does, too. But he doesn't know he's doing it. He thinks we are listening."

Ha ha ha.

"Okay, Karina and Lara, read the next joke, please," the Phonetics professor, Semyon Mikhailovich, said.

Laura read the first line: "What are you doing, my little daughter?"

Karen: "I'm writing a letter to Olya."

Laura: "But you don't know how to write."

Karen: "So what? Olya doesn't know how to read."

Karen stared at Laura for a second with a wry expression in her eyes. Then they both burst out laughing, mostly to please the teacher, but also at the absurdity of the class.

"Very good." Semyon Mikhailovich's eyes danced when he

laughed. He was young, tall, and refined, with dark hair and round black glasses. Laura couldn't be sure if he laughed because he thought the jokes were genuinely funny — in which case, he had the lamest sense of humor ever — or if he saw the absurdity too, and didn't know what else to do but laugh.

Laura wondered if Alyosha had heard that one. She'd tell it to him and see. He probably knew much funnier jokes.

Karen and Laura crossed the crowded hallway to their next class, Translation. Translation was not as much fun as Phonetics.

The professor, Raisa Ivanovna, passed out sheets of onion-skin paper so thin that the O on her typewriter had poked straight through. "Here is your homework for tomorrow. Translate this article into Russian. Let's go over some of the more difficult vocabulary."

Laura glanced at the article, "Siberia: A Land Reborn," and quietly groaned. Karen pointed out one sentence: "The pro-gramme for the economic development of the Baikal-Amur zone, drawn up by scientists of the Siberian branch of the USSR Academy of Sciences, makes up a multivolume encyclopaedia."

"Bedtime reading," Karen whispered.

Raisa Ivanovna explained vocabulary words like *gas reserves* and *hydropower stations*. Laura's mind wandered. This was her last class of the afternoon. As soon as it was over, she would cross the river on her way to meet Alyosha, and they would have their adventure — if she didn't die of boredom first.

★

"Wait." Alyosha stopped her just outside the European Hotel. "What's my name?"

"Oh. Your name. Right." She stopped to consider him in his American down jacket, blue jeans, and oxford cloth shirt. They were Dan's clothes, but he didn't look like a Dan. He looked weirdly preppy.

"You're Skip."

"Skeep? Is that a name?"

"It's a nickname."

"Really? It sounds funny. Okay. I'm Skeep."

"Not Skeep. Skip. Skip."

"Skee-ip."

"Uh, yeah. Leave the talking to me."

She pushed through the revolving door, nodding at the guard just inside. "Passports," he barked.

"Passport. Sure." Laura answered his English with hers, giving the impression of someone who couldn't speak Russian if she tried. She opened her bag and pretended to rummage around for her passport. "We just got into town and I'm so disorganized. . . ."

The guard stared impassively, scrutinizing Alyosha's face and clothes. Laura resisted the temptation to glance back at Alyosha and see how he was holding up under the pressure.

"Here it is." She produced her passport. The guard opened it, studied it, compared the photo to her face, and returned it with a grunt.

"Thank you." She took Alyosha's hand and pulled him inside with her, but the guard said, "Wait. Your passport, please, sir."

Laura hoped the guard didn't notice the flash of panic in Alyosha's eyes. He patted Dan's coat, pretending to search his pockets.

"Did you leave it in the hotel room again, Skip?" Laura scolded. "He keeps doing that. It's gotten us into so much trouble. You'll let us in, won't you? We're just going to spend some money in the Berioska Shop. You know — dollars." She opened her passport case and let a twenty-dollar bill fall to the mosaic floor of the hotel entrance. Whoops, dropped one. She pretended not to notice. "We're leaving town tomorrow, so we've got to get some souvenirs today. I promised my aunt Lucy I'd get her an enamel box, and she'll kill me if I go home without one, right, Skip?"

Alyosha opened his mouth to speak. She could see the *D* of *Da* forming between his teeth. She winced — *no, Alyosha, don't say it. . . .*

He saved himself at the last moment with a silent nod.

The guard subtly stepped on the bill on the floor and waved them inside.

"Thank you! You're a lifesaver. I'll be sure to tell Aunt Lucy how nice you were!" She dragged Alyosha along before the guard could change his mind.

Alyosha's hand, sweaty and shaky, gripped hers. She gave him an encouraging smile, but he stayed stone-faced.

"Don't be nervous," she whispered — sticking with English, just in case — as they crossed the hotel lobby.

"I'm not," he insisted, but she knew he was lying. Being brave for her.

She opened the curtained door to the Berioska Shop, then smiled and waved at the guard who sat just inside. "Hi!" The guard let them pass without a comment. So far, so good.

For one second Alyosha stood frozen in place at the entrance, unsure what to do. He gazed around the gleaming room at the glass cases full of luxurious objects he had no access to. Laura tugged on his hand and pulled him toward the food section.

"Let's go on a binge," she said. "We'll buy whatever you like." She didn't have a lot of money, but this seemed like something worth spending it on.

She took a basket and led him down the aisles of packaged goods, cookies and sardines and tuna and caviar. He seemed afraid to touch anything, so she helped him by taking his hand and forcing it to grip a bottle of olives.

"Laura, I don't like olives," he whispered. The Russian words seemed to spill out of him involuntarily. No one was close enough to hear.

She laughed and put them back. "Ha! Neither do I. What about macadamia nuts?"

"I don't know what those are."

"We'll try them." She put them in the basket. They went to the meat counter. She followed Alyosha's eyes as he took in the varieties of sausages and cutlets and ordered the ones he seemed to linger over.

They bought Dutch cheese, French wine, an amber pin for Alyosha's aunt. Alyosha stared at everything, afraid to say a word. The salesgirls stood around yawning and gossiping, helping out grudgingly when asked.

It's working, Laura thought. *We are actually getting away with this.*

"Okay, Skip — have we got everything we need?"

Alyosha nodded, but his eyes fell on something beyond her shoulder that seemed to trouble him. She turned around. A pretty brunette shopgirl was showing dolls to a German woman. The girl looked at Alyosha curiously, as if she knew him.

"Alyosha?" the shopgirl asked in Russian. "Is that you?"

Alyosha started. Laura pulled him aside. "Who is that?" she whispered in English.

"Marina. I went to school with her," he replied in Russian. When he was nervous, his English failed him. "She recognized me! What are we going to do?"

"Don't worry." She spoke Russian to make sure he understood. "Just keep to the plan. Remember: You are not Alyosha. You're Skip."

"Okay."

The girl — Marina — repeated her question. "Alyosha?"

Laura said in English, "I'm sorry — are you talking to us?"

Marina left the German woman with her dolls and came out from behind the counter. "It is you." She spoke to Alyosha in Russian. "Alyosha, what are you doing here?"

Laura squeezed his hand hard, reminding him not to speak. "We're Americans. Do you speak English?"

"Yes, of course," Marina said. "I'm sorry." She stared at Alyosha, certain she knew him.

"I'm Laura, and this is my friend Skip. He's been sick — laryngitis — so he can't really talk today."

"Oh. I see." Marina stepped back, returning to her professional demeanor. "It's funny, but he looks just like a boy I went to school with. Very much like."

"Really?" Laura faked a light laugh. "That's so funny, because he's not the least bit Russian. He's full-blooded Irish. Skip O'Rourke is his name. His ancestors came from, uh, Tipperary."

Marina looked baffled. The German woman beckoned to her impatiently. "Miss, will you please come back and help me?"

"Excuse me." Marina hurried back to the counter. Alyosha's stiff smile relaxed a bit.

"We'd better get out of here," Laura whispered. She paid for the loot with traveler's checks. As they started out the door, Alyosha stopped, turned, and waved at Marina.

"Good-bye, Marina!" he shouted in Russian. "See you around!"

Laura yanked him away and they ran through the hotel lobby, slowing down to approach the guard at the front door so they wouldn't look suspicious. Safely outside on the street, they ran around the corner, laughing so hard they couldn't breathe.

"I can't believe you did that!" she gasped in English.

"I know," he replied in Russian. "It was foolish."

They had developed a kind of crisis pidgin language, half-English, half-Russian, depending on what popped out of their mouths first. Awkward, but it worked.

Laura walked with him to the metro stop and handed him the fancy plastic Berioska bag. "Your loot, sir." She had learned the Russian word for *loot* from an article they'd read in Translation class on race riots in the US.

"Thank you. Thank you, Laura, for taking a risk with me."

"It was fun."

"Sorry if I ruined everything with Marina, but I couldn't help myself."

"I think we'll be okay."

"You know, I can't enjoy all this food by myself. I think you should come home with me and have some."

"Now?" It was late on a Tuesday afternoon. She had homework to do, and there was a class trip to the ballet that night.

"It's too cold for a picnic in the park," Alyosha said. "But we could have a picnic in my apartment. If you'd like to."

"Well . . ." She made a pretense, to herself, of thinking over his offer. But in reality, she knew exactly what her answer was.

"I *am* in the mood for some macadamia nuts."

"Let's go." He took her hand and led her deep down into the metro. Off they went to Avtovo.

7

★

APARTMENT PICNIC

.

$\mathscr{A}$lyosha lived on the outskirts of the city, the second-to-last metro stop on the Red Line. He led her past an empty supermarket, down a winding path lined with piles of gray snow like Styrofoam, past block after block of run-down apartment towers that looked like housing projects. This part of the city had none of the beauty of downtown Leningrad — no prerevolutionary mansions, no palaces or churches, no river or canals draped with iron filigree bridges. But Alyosha held her hand for the whole walk from the metro, and suddenly Laura loved Avtovo.

They went into one of the high-rise buildings and rode a rickety elevator to the sixth floor. Alyosha kicked aside a wad of greasy paper littering the hallway and unlocked a door: 6A. Laura stepped inside, took a deep breath, and felt immediately at home.

The apartment was small, but neat and cozy. The furniture was simple, but Alyosha had warmed the place up with a red rug on the wooden floor and books and art everywhere. In the hall just inside the door, Alyosha helped her off with her coat and winter boots and gave her a pair of slippers to wear. She followed him down a short hallway past two doors — the toilet and the shower — to the tiny kitchen. He put the Berioska bag on the little kitchen table. She glanced out the window, which looked out at a garbage-strewn lot dotted with an overturned couch, a dresser splintered into pieces, the burned-up frame of a Soviet Fiat.

"Come to the living room. I'll get our picnic ready."

Back up the hall to a larger room, the living room/bedroom, across from the bathroom. The bed, covered in a red wool blanket, was at the back of the room near the window. In the corner stood a drafting table with a ruler, a large drawing pad, and lots of colored pencils and paints. The front of the room was lined with shelves full of books, records, and paintings, with an East German record player holding the place of honor. Three chairs sat around a low coffee table that had been painted blue, trimmed with tiny white flowers.

"It's nice," she said. The Russian words came more easily now that they were relaxed and quiet.

"Sit down anywhere. I'll be right back. Would you like some tea?"

"Yes, please." Instead of sitting, she looked at the photos and paintings that lined the walls. The paintings were precisely rendered scenes of Leningrad street life, full of tiny details: a black cat skulking in the background; an old man's hunched posture; a pinched cigarette burning in a gutter; the porous, shell-chipped texture of an old wall. There were oil portraits of young people who looked like they might be art school friends: an arrogant young man with a walrus mustache and a kerchief around his neck; a beautiful blond boy with full lips and sensitive eyes; two lovely girls, one blonde, one brunette. The brunette was dark and smoky-eyed like a silent film actress, a beret perched jauntily on her wavy hair. The blonde looked bored and naked.

Alyosha returned with a tray of snacks and tea. "Did you paint these?" Laura asked.

"All except those two." He pointed to a watercolor still life of fruit and flowers, and an oil portrait of himself in a style very different from the others — more disjointed and Cubist. "Tanya painted the watercolor, and Roma painted the one of me."

Roma? Tanya? She guessed she'd find out who they were eventually.

He set the tray on the coffee table and nudged it closer to the bed. She reached down and took a handful of macadamia nuts as he showed her the photographs. "This is my school photo from first grade." Six-year-old Alyosha — a red Young Pioneer kerchief knotted around his neck like a Boy Scout tie — grinned at the camera, missing his two front teeth.

"This is Mama and Papa." They posed in a photographer's studio, stiff and gray-haired, a stern, square-jawed man and a woman in her forties with kind eyes like Alyosha's.

"This is my mother with her parents at their dacha, right before the war." His mother, a little girl with a huge white bow in her hair, sat on her father's knee in a blooming garden, while her mother shelled peas into a basket. The little girl and her mother stared solemnly at the camera, but the man smiled with fatherly pride.

"This is my father with his parents during the war." This picture, in grainy black-and-white, was startling. Alyosha's father was a skinny boy of twelve, his pale eyes as large as planets in his shorn skull. His parents were skeletal, eyes shadowed and exhausted. No one smiled. They posed on a rubble-strewn street in Leningrad, a bombed-out building smoking in the background behind them. Passersby walked past the building with barely a look, as if the destruction was nothing unusual, just part of their day. Alyosha's father clutched a ball as if it was the most precious thing he owned, as if that ball could save the world.

Laura had seen pictures of her own parents from this same period — her mother in saddle shoes on a swing with her best friend, her father posing outside his parents' drugstore, a lollipop in his hand — but this looked like a different century, a different universe. Alyosha's father and grandparents looked like refugees, which, in a way, they were. Leningrad was under siege by the Germans at that time, and people were starving and dying by the thousands.

Alyosha plucked an even older photo out from behind this picture. "I hide this picture here," he whispered. "Shhh. Don't tell anyone."

"I won't."

The older picture showed three pampered children in rich satin clothes — two boys and a girl with a little white dog on her lap — posing on a velvet couch before a painting of a man on a horse. "This is my grandmother, my father's mother, as a little girl, with her brothers, before the revolution. Around 1915, I guess. Their father was a merchant. He was killed by the Bolsheviks a few years later and their house was taken by the government and divided into tiny apartments. Grandmother's brothers were killed as well. They let Grandmother live because she pretended to be the family maid."

Laura took the picture from him and stared at it. "That is so sad. But why do you hide the picture?"

"It's not good to have aristocratic roots. You know that."

"But you can't help what your grandparents and great-grandparents were."

Alyosha smirked. "Tell that to the KGB." He replaced the secret picture and took a silver-framed photo down from the shelf. "This is my father as a young navy captain." There was the square-jawed man again, steely blue eyes, in navy whites and a captain's cap with a gold insignia.

"Do you see your parents often?" Laura asked.

Alyosha shook his head. "My mother died a few years ago. And my father isn't speaking to me." He put the photo back on the shelf and sat down to pour out the tea. Laura sat beside him on the bed. She waited for an explanation, but he only smiled wryly and added, "Long story. Let's eat."

He'd made a plate of little open-faced sandwiches: tuna, sardines, a dollop of caviar on a thick bed of butter. The black bread was tangy and chewy. While she tasted the caviar, he put on a record. "Do you like Neil Young?"

"I love him."

"So do I. He is my favorite American rock musician, the greatest."

The warm, rich, funky-sad music filled the room. Alyosha's hand brushed her forearm as he reached for the samovar. The fine hairs near her wrist rose as if pulled by a magnet. She suppressed a shiver and sipped her tea.

They sat quietly listening while Neil sang about how only love can break your heart. "I was whistling this song the other day," Laura said, as if that had been some kind of premonition. Her heartbeat grew heavier, thudding in her chest along with the music. There was an electric tension in the air, magnetizing the foot of space between them so that she felt she couldn't have pulled away from him if she'd wanted to. And she didn't want to.

She wanted to kiss him.

This feeling caught her off guard. She hadn't come to his apartment, as suggestive as that might have sounded, with the intention of kissing anyone. She hardly knew him. She had no idea if he liked her that way.

But there it was. The feeling. Wanting to kiss. Him.

She dared to shift her head the quarter turn it took to face him. His profile was dramatic, almost Roman: a long straight nose, curving lips, deep-set eyes. She was glad he'd shaved off the mustache.

Now his head turned, too. Only inches separated their faces. She felt the faintest trace of his breath on her lips. If she leaned forward just a little bit, her lips would touch his. . . .

Bzzzzt.

The sound jolted both of them, a quick intake of breath, their spines shooting upward, stiffening. "What's that?" she asked.

"The doorbell." He stood up, paused a moment as if he needed to catch his balance, and went to the door. He put his eye to the peephole. "Oh!" He opened the door.

"Hello!" A woman — the dark woman from Alyosha's painting — leaned in to kiss him on each cheek. "Look what I have for you! I wanted to show it to you right away."

"Olga, hello!" Alyosha stepped aside to let her in. She pressed a rectangular package wrapped in rough gray paper into Alyosha's hands, took off her coat, and was unzipping her boots when she finally noticed Laura sitting on the bed in the main room. Laura could almost feel Olga taking in every detail of her hair and clothes as a slow smile spread across Olga's face.

"Hello." She took her time removing her boots and sliding her feet into a pair of slippers. "I'm sorry. I didn't know you had company."

"This is Laura." He led Olga into the main room. "Laura, this is Olga. We're old friends."

"Nice to meet you," Laura said.

"Likewise." Olga took a chair across the table from Laura and reached for a caviar sandwich. "Mmm, so tasty! Sardines! And tuna! Alyosha, where did you get all this?"

"Laura brought it over." Alyosha wasn't going to tell Olga about the Berioska adventure. He must have had his reasons.

Olga eyed Laura with more interest now. "Let me guess. You are Finnish? Or no — German?"

"American," Laura replied.

Olga clapped her hands together. "How exciting! Alyosha, you have a real live American in your apartment!"

Laura tried to interpret Olga's tone. Her voice rose as if she really were excited to see an American, but her sly eyes told a different story.

"I know," Alyosha said with a hint of fatigue.

"And look at you!" She took in Alyosha, still wearing Dan's borrowed American clothes. "Something is very different about you. . . . Are those new Levis?"

"I borrowed them," Alyosha replied.

"Mmm." Olga tossed Laura a meaningful look. "Lyosha, open the package I brought you," she ordered.

Alyosha unwrapped the package. Inside was a book of rock album cover art. "Wow!" He held the shiny book by the edges, as if he didn't want to smudge it with his fingerprints. "Amazing! Olga, where did you get it?"

"One of Roma's contacts. He ran into some British kids and got a real haul in exchange for some of his Soviet army hats. I thought you'd like it."

"It's for me to keep? Thank you!" Alyosha kissed Olga on the cheek, an enthusiastic *smack*.

"I want some tea. Get me a cup?"

"Right away." He scooted into the kitchen.

Olga curled up on her chair like a cat, her feet tucked under her. "So, Laura, is it? Where are you from?"

"Baltimore. It's near Washington, D.C."

"You speak Russian very well. Are you a student?"

"Yes. At the university."

"Hmm. I thought so."

Alyosha returned with a teacup before Laura had a chance to find out what that was supposed to mean.

Olga put the cup under the spout of the samovar and helped herself to tea. "I'm sorry to barge in like this, Alyosha. I didn't think —"

"It's okay —" Alyosha began.

Laura rose to her feet. "I've got to get back to the dorm anyway. We're going to the ballet tonight."

"Oh?" Olga asked. "What are you seeing?"

"I think it's *Swan Lake*."

Olga grinned. "What else?" She took another sandwich.

Alyosha walked Laura to the door. "That was fun today," he said quietly.

"Yes. We'll have to do it again sometime, Skip."

"I don't know about that. Marina might not let us get away next time." He rested his hand on her lower back, then took it away quickly, as if suddenly realizing what he was doing, and reached for her coat. "Call me again soon?"

"I will." She shrugged into her coat, shoved her feet into her boots, pulled on her hat. Alyosha opened the door for her. She lingered in the doorway. Something was called for, a gesture of some kind, a kiss. But now was not the time.

"Nice to meet you!" Olga half turned and waved, her mouth full.

"Nice to meet you, too." Laura stepped into the hallway with one last look at Alyosha. She was leaving him behind with Olga, who was . . . *what* to him, exactly?

"See you soon." He closed the door.

She rode the elevator down and found her way back to the metro. The neighborhood looked less appealing in the gloom.

8

★

PARTY AT ALYOSHA'S

*H*ow did the Berioska heist go?"

She met Dan in his robe and flip-flops, a towel slung over his shoulder, on his way back from the shower. His curly hair was damp and his glasses slightly fogged. Unlike Laura, he'd skipped the ballet.

"We almost got caught. One of the salesgirls recognized him from school."

"Bummer."

"But we managed to escape without getting arrested."

"Thank God for that. Hate to see you sent to the gulag for helping a Russkie impersonate an American."

"Yeah, that probably wouldn't be worth it."

Dan stopped in front of his room. "Care to come in? Sergei's upstairs and I'm practically naked. All I have to do is let this pesky bathrobe fall to the floor and —"

Laura laughed. "I should get to bed —"

"That's exactly what I'm suggesting." He opened the door and stepped aside to usher her in. She shook her head.

"I must be crazy to resist such a tempting offer, but not tonight."

"Okay. Your loss." He tossed his towel on a chair. "Do you have my clothes?"

Right — the clothes she'd lent to Alyosha for the heist. He'd still been wearing them when she'd left. An image of them tossed to the floor — mingled with Olga's wool skirt and sweater — flashed involuntarily through her mind. Highly unpleasant. She shoved the image away.

"Sorry — Alyosha still has them. I'll get them back as soon as I can."

"All right, but don't take too long. That was my only pair of sneakers." Dan picked up the towel and rubbed his wet hair. "Sure you don't want to come in? Last chance . . ."

She shook her head, smiling, and walked back to her room. Nina's corner was dark, her slow, heavy breathing the only sound. Karen was in bed, reading in a pool of light from her lamp. When Laura walked in, she raised her eyebrows to indicate the unspoken question: *Well?*

Laura shrugged, hoping it conveyed the unspoken answer of *So-so*. The heist had been fun, but she would have liked to have ended the day differently. Like, without another girl in the room.

She changed into her pajamas and sat with Karen on her bed.

"I'm a little surprised to see you tonight," Karen whispered. "I thought you might . . . you know . . ."

"We did go back to Alyosha's apartment," Laura said. "But he had an unexpected visitor."

Karen waited to hear more.

"All I know is that her name's Olga, and she's a friend from art school."

"Friend? Or girlfriend? Or former girlfriend?"

"No idea. She's got some kind of claim on him, though. She's very comfortable in his apartment."

"Hmm. Are you going to call him again?"

"He asked me to."

"Do you like him?"

Laura thought of Alyosha's profile, so close as they sat together on his bed. The way the curve of his nose seemed to point to his curling lips, saying, *Look*.

"I have to find out more," she said.

"Then call him," Karen advised.

Laura went to her own bed. Karen turned off the light. "Good night."

"Good night."

Laura lay awake in the dark, blinking at the ceiling. Across the room, she heard Nina sigh and roll over in her sleep.

"Good night, American girls," Nina muttered.

Laura went to the usual phone booth after classes on Monday afternoon. It was deepest February, the snow banked high along the streets. As she stepped inside the booth, she noticed him again: the same man in the fur hat and black glasses who'd been there before, walking his dog.

He must live around here, she thought. *I keep coming to call Alyosha at the same time of day, after classes . . . and that just happens to be when he walks his dog.*

A reasonable explanation. But still.

He's already seen me here in the phone booth. And he can't hear what I'm saying from across the street. So I might as well go ahead and make the call.

But she resolved to walk to another phone booth, even farther away, the next time, in case the man decided to follow her. Did he know she was American? She wasn't trading on the black market like Donovan. But a lot of students did, and she'd heard that the Soviet authorities sometimes sent out undercover agents to stop it.

She dialed Alyosha and was glad to hear his voice when he picked up.

"Laura! I'm so happy you called. Olga had a great idea. I'm having a party on Friday night, so you can meet my friends. Will you come?"

So he was having a party, but it was Olga's idea? That sounded like a girlfriend move. Still, he was inviting her. And Olga wanted her there . . . but that might just be for the social coup. She knew some Russians liked to show off their Western friends at parties, as a status symbol. If only it were that easy to be cool at home.

She'd never understand what was going on if she didn't go.

"Yes, I'd like to come," she said. "Can I bring one of my friends?"

"American or Russian?"

"American."

"Of course! Yes. All Americans welcome. Russians must pass a security clearance first."

"I don't really know any other Russians, Alyosha. My roommate Nina is Ukrainian. But she's no fun at parties."

"Well, on Friday night you will meet many more Russians, and they are all fun at parties. Who are you bringing?"

"My roommate Karen."

"The *negrityanka*? Really?" She had mentioned Karen in one of their talks, how she was stared at more than any of the other Americans because she was black and cut her hair in a short, new-wave flattop that Russians — even complete strangers — were always trying to touch. Karen looked kind of like the disco goddess Grace Jones — if Grace Jones wore glasses and went to Oberlin.

"Yes. Is that all right?"

"That's fantastic! Extremely wonderful! Wait until my friends hear. They will meet a real American *negrityanka* in my home!"

"Yeah, it's thrilling all right." Laura muttered in English. Her Russian wasn't quite good enough to convey her mixed feelings. She worried now about how comfortable Karen would feel. But Karen was getting used to being seen as exotic.

"What did you say?" Alyosha asked.

"I said, it will be a big excitement," Laura replied, returning to Russian.

"Indeed. Come at seven. See you Friday."

"See you then. Good-bye, Alyosha."

"Good-bye, Laura. I'll anxiously await you on Friday."

She hung up. Friday! It was only Monday. Why didn't he want to get together for coffee or something sooner?

The man with the dog had crossed the street and was walking past the phone booth just then. She waited until he reached the next corner, then she stepped out. When she got to the corner he was gone.

Laura and Karen rode the steep escalator down into the Gostinii Dvor Metro Station, as noble workers fighting for freedom glared down at them fiercely from a gigantic stained-glass mural. It was like descending into an underground palace. The gold-and-marble walls of the metro platform gleamed in the light of crystal chandeliers.

"Have you ever been to New York?" Karen asked. "Because this is not what the subway looks like in New York."

The last time Laura had been in the New York subway, a rat had run over her foot.

The train arrived with a quiet *whoosh* and they got on, carefully watching the stops to Avtovo. Laura felt all eyes in the car on them, and especially on Karen. Some people looked away when she challenged them by glaring back, but others stared openly and shamelessly.

It was a long ride to Avtovo. They ascended and walked along a rutted road of frozen mud, past the decrepit grocery store with cans of beets arranged pyramid-style in the window. Five stories above them, a woman with a scarf in her hair and fat arms dumped the contents of a trash can into a courtyard.

"Is that allowed?" Karen dodged a rotten cabbage.

Laura shrugged. "Think of the garbage as adding color to the landscape."

"Remind me again: Who's going to be here tonight?" Karen asked. "Besides your friend Alyosha, I mean." Her friend Alyosha. She couldn't claim that he was more than a friend, not yet. But she was hoping, maybe . . .

"Olga, who he knows from art school. And some other friends. He didn't specify. But he seems to run with an arty crowd."

"Okay. That's good."

Laura felt Karen trying to catch her eye. She kept her gaze glued to the sidewalk.

"Afraid you're going to slip on the ice?" Karen asked.

"A little."

"No you're not."

Laura gave in and looked up. Karen wanted to ask her something annoying. She could feel it. There was no escape.

"Exactly what are you hoping will happen at this party?" Karen asked. "I mean, should I expect to go back to the dorm by myself, or —"

"No! Alyosha's a friend, like you said. Besides, we have to get back for curfew. The rules and all."

"Right, the rules."

"But . . . do you ever find these Russians hard to read?"

"Totally," Karen said. "There's the language problem of course — I know I'm missing all these subtleties, jokes and things just flying over my head. But their relationships are so dramatic! All their friendships look like love to me. Boys and girls, boys and boys, girls and girls, children and their grandmas — all so romantic. So touchy-feely."

"I know! They're always kissing. I can't tell what's what."

"Spill it, Reid," Karen said. "What's really on your mind?"

"Nothing. I'm telling you the facts to the best of my knowledge," Laura insisted. "Everything beyond that is pure speculation."

"I speculate that you have the hots for this Alyosha guy."

"Pure speculation . . ."

They wove their way along cement paths lined with dirty snow until they found Alyosha's address. Laura was about to press the buzzer for his apartment when Karen pointed out that the door was propped open. They went inside and found the elevator waiting.

"It smells like pee in here," Karen whispered.

The elevator rattled to the sixth floor. Laura paused in front of Alyosha's door and took a deep breath. "Ready?"

"Ready."

She knocked. Alyosha threw open the door and grinned. He wore Dan's jeans and a T.Rex T-shirt.

"My guests of honor are here! You're the first ones to arrive."

"Really? But you said seven o'clock."

"I know, I know. My friends are always late. Come in. Let me take your coats." They went inside. The Beatles were playing on the turntable.

"This is Karen Morrison," Laura said. "Karen, Alyosha."

Alyosha shook her hand and said in English, "So pleasure to meet you."

Karen smiled. "So pleasure to meet you, too."

Laura presented him with a bottle of Georgian wine. "Lovely! Thank you! Thank you!" Alyosha rubbed his hands together and took the wine into the kitchen. "Sit down! I bring out *zakuski.*"

Laura led Karen into the main room, set up for a party with extra chairs. Laura sat on the bed while Karen flipped through Alyosha's record collection.

"Does he have this place all to himself?" Karen asked in a low voice.

"I think so," Laura said. She hadn't given it much thought, but Karen's surprise made her wonder. There was a housing shortage in Leningrad. Karen had been telling Laura about her friend Natia, a Georgian artist she'd met at a poetry reading, who was divorced but still lived with her husband because he had nowhere else to go. They shared a communal apartment with two other families. Most of the other people she'd met lived in *kommunalki*, too. Having an apartment all to yourself was a privilege — or a piece of great good luck. How had Alyosha — a sign painter for movie theaters — gotten so lucky?

He carried in a plate of pickles, cheese, and bread; the wine; and three glasses. He poured some wine and gave each girl a glass. "A toast. To our friendship."

Friendship. Laura checked a wince at the word, and on Karen's meaningful glance sent back a psychic message: *pure speculation.*

"To friendship." They clinked glasses and drank. The doorbell rang.

Alyosha sprang to the door and soon ushered in Olga, dark eyes heavily lined in black pencil and carrying a bouquet of flowers. Laura caught Karen's eye: *That's her.*

"Lyosha, dear!" *Kiss, kiss.* "I found daisies! This time of year! Am I the first to arrive? I'll get a vase. . . ."

She marched toward the kitchen with a glance into the living room. "Girls! Hello! I'll be right there."

Another look — sympathetic — passed between Laura and Karen. Why did the sight of Olga send Laura's mood plummeting? It wasn't as if she hadn't expected to see her.

"Now we have a party!" Alyosha rubbed his hands together with gusto. "Where's Roma?"

"Right behind me!" Olga called from the kitchen.

A stocky young man with a bushy mustache and thick hair, like Stalin's, burst through the door and grabbed Alyosha by the shoulders. "Aaaach!" he grunted happily, waving a bottle of vodka. "Alyosha, my friend." He gave Alyosha a smacking kiss on each cheek.

"This is Olga's husband, Roma," Alyosha said to Karen and Laura.

Laura's spirits suddenly rose as she and Karen went to greet him. "Olga's husband! How nice," Karen said.

"This is Karen, and this is Laura," Alyosha told Roma.

"The American girls!" Kisses all around. "Olga and I went to art school with Alyosha," Roma explained.

Olga came out of the kitchen with the vase of flowers. "I spent more time posing than painting." It sounded like she was bragging. She set the flowers on the table and took the vodka from Roma to put it on ice.

"She posed for all of us," Roma added. "But she was Alyosha's favorite model."

"After Tanya," Olga said with a flirtatious bat her of eyelashes.

Laura was tempted to ask, "Who's Tanya?" but Olga's tone made her bite her tongue. She didn't want to hear the answer from Olga.

The doorbell rang again and two more men came in, introduced as Vova and Grisha. Vova was blond and cute, with a trim beard. Laura caught Karen checking him out.

Everyone chattered and laughed in Russian. Laura sipped a small glass of vodka, struggling to keep up with the conversation. It went faster than she was used to, peppered with unfamiliar slang and expressions she didn't understand. She glanced at Karen, who looked a little blank, too.

Roma refilled Laura's and Karen's shot glasses with vodka. "Don't sip it," he warned. "That's how you get sick. Down it all at once — *oop-ah!*" He threw his head back and tossed down another shot to demonstrate. "Go on, girls. *Oop-ah!*"

Laura looked to Karen, but she was no help, saying, "Come on, girl. *Oop-ah!*" They clinked glasses and drank their shots in one gulp. Laura gasped and reached for a slice of cucumber. She felt a surge of warmth.

Alyosha turned his Neil Young record over and "Southern Man" played. "I heard Kukharsky sing this song at Café Bluebird," Vova said.

"He sang Neil Young in public?" Grisha asked. "And it was okay?"

"I hate Neil Young," Olga said. "His voice is whiny."

"This song is government approved," Vova said.

"Because it criticizes the American South," Karen guessed. "I can see why they'd like it."

"Exactly." Vova nodded.

"Alyosha, take this whining record off and put on the Beatles." Olga pouted.

"It will be over in a minute," Roma said. "Did you girls know that the Beatles played a secret concert here in 1970?"

"It was 1969," Alyosha said.

"I heard '68," Vova said.

"What happened?" Laura had never heard this story.

"Their plane landed at Pulkovo" — the Leningrad airport — "very briefly," Roma explained. "And the Beatles climbed out onto the wing and played three songs."

"With acoustic guitars," Alyosha added.

"Very fast, before the guards snapped out of their stupors and stopped them," Vova finished.

"Wow," Karen said.

"It isn't true," Olga said.

"It is," Vova insisted. "My friend Kolya saw the concert himself."

"The Beatles were very taboo back then," Grisha said. "My uncle was kicked out of the university just for having a Beatles tape in his room."

"They're more tolerated now," Vova said. "A little bit."

"The police used to arrest guys for having long hair," Roma said. "They'd arrest you and cut your hair, then let you go. After giving you a scare."

"They still do that sometimes," Alyosha said.

"Not as much," Vova said. "But sometimes."

Olga feigned a yawn. "Let's talk about something else."

Her eyes took in Laura's corduroys and Karen's jeans, their bulky sweaters. "What are they wearing in America these days, girls?"

Karen shrugged. "This, I guess."

Olga scowled, not believing her.

"Have you heard this one, girls?" Grisha asked. "A man walks into a butcher shop and asks, 'Do you have any fish?'" The Russians laughed in anticipation of a punch line they already knew. "So the butcher says, 'Here we don't have any meat. Fish they don't have across the street!'"

Everyone laughed and toasted Grisha. Laura started gulping mineral water; the toasts were catching up to her.

"Now tell us an American joke," Vova said.

Laura tried to think of a joke that would work in Russian, but all the ones she thought of depended on plays on English words, like "Because Seven ate Nine" or "I left my harp in Sam Clam's disco."

"Here's one," Karen said. "But I think it will only work in English."

"Go ahead," Alyosha said. "I'll translate."

"Okay." Karen cleared her throat and said in English: "A nose walks into a bar and asks for a drink. The bartender says, 'Sorry, I can't serve you. You're already off your face.'"

Laura laughed. The Russians gave her blank stares.

Karen tried to explain in Russian. "See, in English *off your face* is slang for *drunk*. . . . I thought you might understand because of the Gogol story, you know, 'The Nose'? Where a man's nose detaches from his face and walks around town . . . ?" Karen trailed off.

The Russians nodded. "Oh yes! Gogol. Great story."

Karen sighed. "Jokes never work if you have to explain them."

Alyosha got up and slapped Karen on the back. "No, no! It was funny! Very, very funny."

He went into the kitchen to get more food. When he came back, he squeezed next to Laura on the bed. Their arms touched, elbow to shoulder. Karen sat on her left side and their arms were touching, too, but somehow it didn't have the same electric feeling. Vova was on Karen's left, but their arms weren't touching . . . yet.

Olga grabbed Alyosha's guitar and put it in his hands. "Sing us a song, Lyosha." Now she squeezed onto the bed, close to Alyosha. The bed was crowded. There were two empty chairs across the table. Roma and Grisha looked lonely.

"Olga, come back and sit in your chair," Roma said.

"You're not my boss," Olga snapped.

"I'm your husband," Roma shot back. "That means I am your boss."

"Okay, then, prove it. Make me move."

The Neil Young record chose that moment to cut off. In the tense silence that followed Olga's challenge, Laura heard the click of the needle arm settling into its saddle. To cut the tension, Alyosha strummed the guitar.

"Move over, Olga," he said, softly but firmly. "I don't have room to hold the guitar."

Olga stormed out of the room. The bathroom door slammed.

Alyosha stretched out his arm and began to strum for real.

"I didn't know you played the guitar," Laura said.

"There is so much you don't know about me." He smiled enigmatically.

"Hey — there's a lot you don't know about her, too," Karen put in a little too forcefully. The vodka made her louder than usual. "Did you know Laura has a black belt in karate?"

"What?" Laura said.

"Is that true?" Grisha asked.

"No, it's not true," Laura told him.

"I'm just trying to buff up your image," Karen said.

"You don't need to do that," Alyosha said. "Her image is nice enough already."

Laura turned toward him, surprised but pleased. She pressed her arm against his. He pressed back. All the vodka warmth seemed to concentrate in that arm.

Olga returned from the bathroom and took her seat next to Roma as if nothing had happened. Alyosha launched into the first chords of a song everyone but Karen and Laura seemed to know. Soon all the Russians were singing an old folk song. Laura managed to catch a few phrases: "It's evening, I couldn't sleep . . . I tossed and turned, I had a dream . . . someone interpreted my dream and said . . . you will lose your wild head."

"That is beautiful," she said when it was finished.

"It's called 'Stenka Razin's Dream.'" Alyosha sang it again slowly, while Grisha explained the words as best he could in English. Stenka Razin was kind of a Cossack Robin Hood, who dreamed that his horse bucked and danced and went wild underneath him. A colonel told him that the dream foretold his death. "You will lose your wild, untamed head," he predicted. Then an evil wind blew from the east and knocked Stenka's hat off his wild, untamed head.

"Guess who I saw the other day, Lyosha," Olga said. "Speaking of wild and untamed. Tanya."

That name again — Olga seemed to love to bring up Tanya. Alyosha looked down, nodding, and Roma, Vova, and Grisha stopped clapping and joking. An inch of space suddenly materialized between Laura's shoulder and Alyosha's.

"Well, how is she?" Roma asked. "You didn't tell me this before."

"I didn't speak to her," Olga said. "I saw her come out of the Hotel Astoria and get into a car. She glanced at me but didn't say hello. I know she saw me but she pretended she didn't see me. Why would she do that?"

Alyosha plucked distractedly at one string of his guitar.

"Who's Tanya?" Laura asked.

"An old friend of Alyosha's," Roma said.

"An old girlfriend," Olga corrected.

"Oh." Laura glanced at Karen.

"Here's a picture of her." Olga got up and rummaged through some of Alyosha's paintings until she found a portrait of a beautiful blue-eyed blonde with bare shoulders.

"Olga, put that away." Alyosha thrust the guitar into Roma's hands and snatched the painting from Olga. Too late, though: Laura had already seen it. The blonde was the same girl she'd seen in a nude painting earlier. So that was Tanya.

Roma strummed the chords of a Beatles song. "Let's sing something the American girls know."

Alyosha set the painting down, facing the wall. He was scowling. A triumphant smile played on Olga's lips.

If she's trying to make me jealous, it's not working, Laura said to herself. But it was working a little bit.

"Come on, girls, sing!" Grisha keened out "And I Love Her" in a nasal Russian accent. Laura and Karen belted it out along with him. It felt good to sing in English, to know the words.

Next, Roma started strumming a song that was eerily familiar to Laura. She wasn't sure at first what it was, but she knew she knew it in some deep, unconscious way, the way you know songs that you've heard on the radio or in the supermarket your whole life without ever really listening to them.

"You know what this is, don't you?" Karen grinned at her mischievously.

"It's so familiar. . . ." Laura strained to catch the melody in her memory.

The Russians came to the chorus, and at last she recognized it.

Feelings! Whoa whoa whoa feelings . . . whoa whoa whoa feelings . . . Again in my heart . . .

"Oh my God, I hate this song," Laura said to Karen in English.

"But right now, you're loving it," Karen said. "Aren't you?"

"Sort of."

"That's a great song," Grisha said. "I love that song."

Karen and Laura looked at each other and laughed.

"What is so funny?" Vova asked. "It's American pop. Super fantastic."

Karen suddenly grabbed Laura's wrist and looked at her watch. "Whoa! What time is it? Eleven o'clock!"

"We missed curfew," Laura said. They'd been told they could get sent home for missing curfew. But surely they were allowed one mistake. . . .

"What time does the metro stop running?" Karen asked.

"Midnight," Alyosha said.

Laura and Karen stood up, and Laura said, "We better run. Sorry to leave so suddenly, but we're supposed to be in our dorm by ten."

They kissed everyone good-bye and promised more parties soon. Alyosha helped them into their coats and showed them to the door.

"I'll walk you to the metro," he said.

"We can find it," Karen said. Laura was getting a wave of *hurry hurry hurry* from her — she really didn't want to get caught breaking curfew.

Laura knew she had to go, but she wanted to stay. She hadn't gotten the answer she'd come for. She'd met Alyosha's friends, but what did that mean? Had he simply wanted to show off the random American girl he'd met, a foreign curiosity? Or was he trying to show *her* something about who he was, to bring her into his life?

It was hard to tell. But they had to leave. Karen tugged on her elbow.

"Thank you, Alyosha," Laura said. "It was wonderful!" She offered him one last opening. "See you again?"

"Call me soon." Alyosha kissed her once on each cheek. He hesitated for a second, then impulsively kissed her lightly on the lips. "I wish you didn't have to leave."

An answer at last. Not to every question, but to the one question that had most been on Laura's mind. She still didn't want to leave, but now she could go with a lighter heart.

"Soon," she told him, and tried not to feel too disappointed when the door had to close.

The girls ran out into the frigid night, all the way to the metro, and caught the last train back to the center of town. "Shoot," Laura said as they took a seat in the half-empty car. "I forgot to get Dan's clothes back."

"Dan can kiss those clothes good-bye," Karen said. "And he knows it." The lights of the subway tunnel flashed across her face. "So what was going on between Olga and Alyosha?"

"I have no idea. Do you think she's in love with him?"

"I don't know," Karen said. "But that whole thing with Tanya? You got what Olga was hinting at, didn't you?" On seeing Laura's blank look, she added, "When she said she saw Tanya coming out of the Astoria. A foreigner's hotel. She was implying that Tanya's a prostitute."

"What? That's a pretty big leap."

"Natia told me, and I think it's true," Karen said. "You know how they say if a Russian is willing to go into our dorm it means he's either KGB or a dissident so desperate he has nothing to lose?"

Laura nodded. Their chaperones, Dr. Stein and Dr. Durant, had warned them about this.

"According to Natia, you can also add that a Russian woman hanging around a tourist hotel is either a tour guide, an informant, or a hooker."

"So maybe Tanya's a tour guide."

"Maybe. But Olga's tone suggested otherwise."

"So you're saying Alyosha's ex-girlfriend is a hooker."

"I'm not saying that — Olga is."

Was Olga trying to hurt Alyosha, or was she telling the truth? And what did it matter? Alyosha couldn't control his ex-girlfriend's actions.

"Whatever. I don't care."

The walk from the metro stop to the dorm felt endless. The night air had a bone-rattling dampness, a frozen fog that enveloped them as they walked, filled their lungs and made it hard to breathe. At last they reached Dorm Number Six. The guard's light was out. It was midnight.

"We're going to catch hell for this," Karen predicted.

"What are we going to do?" Laura asked.

"You want to sleep outside tonight? We're going to wake up Ivan."

They pressed the buzzer and waited. Nothing happened for a while. They rang again. A light came on, and soon the door was opened by old Ivan, who scowled at them in his nightshirt and felt slippers.

"You're late," he grumbled, locking the door behind them as they scurried inside and tried to warm up. "I'll have to report you."

"We're sorry! We're sorry!" the girls cried. "It won't happen again."

"That's right, it won't," Ivan said. "Next time I won't let you in. Good night." He stomped away into the back room where he slept.

They ran upstairs to their room. "He didn't stop in the office to write down our names," Karen whispered. "Maybe he won't report us."

"Maybe by morning he'll think he dreamed the whole thing,"

Laura said. "And now to deal with the wrath of Nina." Donovan had told them that all the Soviet roommates in their dorm had been specially chosen for their willingness to report on the foreign students' activities, and Laura had no reason to doubt him. She was beginning to see that reporting on neighbors greased the gears that made the Soviet system work.

They opened their door slowly and quietly. The room was dark.

"She's asleep," Laura whispered.

They undressed in the dark and got into bed. Like magic, the spot where Alyosha had kissed her was still warm on Laura's lips. The long walk in the cold hadn't made it go away. Nothing could make that feeling go away.

"Stenka Razin's Dream" drifted through her mind as she fell asleep: "You're going to lose your wild head . . ."

Too late, she thought sleepily. *My wild head is lost.*

9

★

WINTER IN THE SUMMER GARDEN

*L*aura opened her eyes the next morning to find Nina already up, sipping tea and studying. Karen snored softly in her bed. Laura turned over. Nina looked up.

"Oh. You are awake," Nina said coldly.

"Mm-hmm." Laura sat up and rubbed her eyes. Her tongue was a wool sock, and tiny elves seemed to be hacking at the backs of her eyes with mini icepicks. Karen stirred at the sound of their voices.

"You missed breakfast this morning," Nina said.

"Oh no," Laura said. "What will I do without my morning gruel?" Breakfast in the university cafeteria consisted of weak coffee, strong tea, and gloppy gray kasha. That beat lunch, which, last time Laura had bothered to show up, featured fish head soup and mystery meat. It was best to stick with black bread and margarine.

Nina's face showed no reaction beyond an almost

imperceptible narrowing of the eyes. She slurped her tea. Karen lifted her head.

"What? What?" She looked around the room, smiled at Laura, let her head fall back on her pillow. "Morning, girlies. I'm too sleepy to speak Russian."

"I'm glad you are finally awake, Karen." Nina may not have understood Karen's English, but in any case she ignored it and plowed ahead in Russian. "I have something to say, and this way I can say it to both of you at the same time. I will not have to repeat myself."

Laura sat up and slid her feet into her slippers. "Can it wait just one minute while I run to the bathroom?"

"It won't take long," Nina said.

Sadist, Laura thought.

"I went to bed at eleven o'clock last night and the two of you were not home yet. I don't know how you got in after curfew but I'm glad you did. I'd hate for you to freeze to death on the street. I know that happens often to homeless people in America, but we don't allow it here."

Laura and Karen blinked at her, too sleepy to argue, just wanting the lecture to end so they could get on with their lives.

"The rules are very clear," Nina said. "You must sleep here in the dorm every night. You must be in your room by ten o'clock each night. If you're not, I'm supposed to report you. If the university wants a reason to send you home, they can use this."

"We're sorry, Nina," Karen said.

"Yes, we're sorry." Laura hoped that would satisfy her.

"I like you," Nina said. "I want to be friends."

"So do we!" Karen said. "We just lost track of time, and, uh, the metro was late."

"The metro is never late."

Laura couldn't argue with that — she'd never known the metro to be anything but punctual. "We won't do it again, Nina."

"We promise," Karen said.

"All right," Nina said. "I will make you some tea." She stood up and moved out of the room with a cowlike slowness that had an odd, heavy grace.

"Close one." Karen sat up and switched into English. "I have a hangover."

"Me too." Laura could still taste the vodka in the pores of her tongue. She remembered Alyosha's kiss and touched that spot on her lips. Still warm. She pulled on her robe and snatched her towel off the armoire door for the trip down the hall to the bathroom.

She passed Nina in the kitchen, gossiping by the stove with Alla, Binky's roommate. On her way back from the toilets, she spotted Ilona slipping out of Dan and Sergei's room, her blond hair very mussed. Hmm ... Dan or Sergei? Laura suspected Dan. He was deceptively suave for a skinny geek in John Lennon wire-rims.

Laura returned to the room to find the table set with three glasses of tea and three small bowls of oatmeal. "It's like the

Three Bears' house," Laura said. Nina didn't get it. "Where did the oatmeal come from?"

"Alla's roommate . . . Pinky?"

"Binky."

"She gave this to Alla, who shared it with me. It's from America. Magic oatmeal."

"Magic?" Laura tasted it. Apple cinnamon. "You mean, instant?"

"Yes. It's good, no?"

"Very good. Thank you, Nina."

"A peace offering," Nina said.

Karen caught Laura's eye. Peace offering, or bait to lull them into complacency? Laura knew Karen was suspicious. But what could they do? It was oatmeal. It tasted good. They ate it.

A few days later, Alyosha invited her to go for a walk. She set out on the tram for their usual meeting spot.

She nabbed a seat next to a young woman. A man stood in the aisle next to her, hanging on to the strap. He was dark and goateed and wore a fake-leather racing jacket. Something about him made her think of Atlantic City and cheap casinos. He winked at her. A gold tooth flashed when he smiled.

Laura looked away, determined not to meet his eye again. She was against winking as a general principle, but in this case it was especially unnerving. What did a wink mean? It could mean anything from "Hey, baby" to "I know what you're up to and you've got nowhere to hide."

"You speak English?" the man asked in heavily accented English. "Where you from?"

She ignored him, but he wouldn't stop. "From England? From Germany? From France?"

The woman next to Laura got up, and the man took over her empty seat. "You very pretty." He pawed at her glove. "I kiss your hand."

She yanked her hand away. "No! Please leave me alone."

"America? You from America?"

"Yes, okay?" She tried to be polite, but she didn't understand what he wanted with her. She got off the tram before her stop but it was no use — he followed her off and dogged her down Nevsky Prospekt. She had to lose him. Whatever was going on with this strange man, she didn't want to get Alyosha involved.

"Come to bar with me, yes? We practice English."

"I can't," she said in Russian. "I'm meeting someone."

"Please," he said. "I'm nice guy. I must talk to you. I'm in trouble!"

Great, he was in trouble. Whatever that meant — if it was true — it was sure to mean trouble for her, too.

But what if he really needed her help? She looked at him, but was quickly overcome by waves of skeeviness like cheap cologne. She couldn't help him. He might not be in trouble at all.

"I'm sorry."

He tugged at her elbow. "Please! Stop and listen to me for one minute!"

She was desperate to get rid of him. They approached the European Hotel and suddenly she knew how. She nodded at the uniformed guard out front and pushed her way through the gleaming glass doors. Inside, another guard stopped her. "Passport, please."

She showed him her passport. "Are you a guest in the hotel?" he asked.

"Yes," she lied. The guard stepped aside to let her into the lobby. She glanced back through the door. The strange man paced outside the hotel. How long would he wait for her there? If he hung out in front of a foreigners' hotel for too long, he'd look very suspicious . . . unless he was KGB, in which case he could do whatever he wanted.

She sat down in the lobby to wait him out. The desk clerk squinted at her. She smiled and nodded at him as if she were completely at ease. She watched the guests come and go: a sleek German couple in expensive coats, four ratty British students underdressed for the cold, and a tall, handsome, oddly familiar-looking man with gray-blond hair . . . Who was he? When he spoke to the clerk in a crisp English accent she recognized him as an actor she'd seen on *Masterpiece Theater.*

She considered the skeevy guy waiting outside for her. What did he want? He might be a black marketeer, hoping to get jeans or dollars from her. He might be on the make, trying to pick up girls. He could be a dissident genuinely in trouble, but she didn't see how she could help him if he was. He could simply be crazy. Or he could be a KGB agent trying to get information from her. Donovan, the cowboy drug dealer, claimed that every American student had a KGB agent assigned to follow him or her.

If that was true, her agent must be bored out of his mind.

Or maybe not. Maybe Alyosha was not who he said he was. Maybe he was her KGB agent. After all, he had that nice apartment all to himself. . . .

Laura went to the door to see if the coast was clear. The stalker was gone.

She continued down Nevsky Prospekt to the bookstore, turning around every so often to make sure the man wasn't following her. The street was so crowded, it was hard to tell for sure. But she didn't see him.

Alyosha was waiting for her in Poetry, just like before. Today he was reading Marina Tsvetaeva.

"Sorry I'm late," she said. "Some guy was following me."

"A guy? What guy?" He made her describe how the man had acted and tell her everything that had happened. When they walked out onto the street, he looked around carefully.

"Do you see him?" he asked.

"No. He's gone."

Alyosha frowned. "What did he look like?"

She described his scruffy goatee, his vinyl jacket, his gold tooth . . .

"What does it mean?" she asked.

"I don't know. Probably nothing."

They stood on the street for a few minutes, letting the crowd jostle them. Alyosha eyed everyone who passed by. Laura lifted her face to the pale, weak sunlight. In another hour it would be dark.

"It's not so horribly cold today," she said. The clock down the street said the temperature was -10 Celsius.

Alyosha jiggled his hands in his pockets. "Let's go for a walk."

He led her up Nevsky Prospekt toward the Hermitage. They stopped to buy ice cream from a cart on the street. The ice cream was not quite white and not quite brown, not quite vanilla and not at all chocolate.

"What flavor is this?" Laura asked.

Alyosha shrugged. "What do you mean? It's ice cream." He tasted his cone. "It's cream flavored."

In Decemberists' Square, they admired the statue of Peter the Great, founder of St. Petersburg. Alyosha mumbled some words under his breath.

"What are you doing?" Laura asked.

Alyosha blushed. "Nothing. Just reciting some lines from a poem we learned in school."

"What poem? Let me hear it."

"No. I don't like it. But I've been so programmed I can hardly walk past this damn statue without muttering the words."

"Let me hear them. Please."

He recited:

Miracle and beauty of the North,
Arose in pride and stood in splendor
Both from the darkness of the woods
And from the swamps of endless marshes . . .

"We were just reading that in Translation class," Laura said. "It's that Pushkin poem about Peter the Great."

"We memorized a lot of poetry in school," Alyosha said. "Memorizing and reciting was practically all we did."

"I hardly know any poetry by heart. Just one Emily Dickinson poem I memorized once when I was too heartbroken to do anything else."

"Which one?"

She recited in English: "'After great pain, a formal feeling comes . . .'" She stopped, embarrassed. "Now I know why you felt shy about it."

"Keep going. I like the sound of it."

After great pain, a formal
*   feeling comes —*
The Nerves sit ceremonious,
*   like Tombs —*
The stiff Heart questions was
*   it He, that bore,*

And Yesterday, or Centuries
        before?

The Feet, mechanical, go
        round —
Of Ground, or Air, or
        Ought —
A Wooden way
Regardless grown,
A Quartz contentment, like a
        stone —

This is the Hour of Lead —
Remembered, if outlived,
As Freezing persons, recollect
        the Snow —
First — Chill — then Stupor —
        then the letting go —

Clouds had rolled in off the Baltic Sea, and the sky had grayed since they left Dom Knigi. They stared at the leaden river.

"That poem could have been written here," Alyosha said. "It could be by Anna Akhmatova, feeling suicidal during an endless Leningrad winter, or during the siege. What made you memorize it?"

"A sad winter. Probably not as sad as the German siege, though."

He laughed. "I hope not."

"Yes, definitely not as sad as that." She told him about that sophomore winter, a year before, when she went home to Baltimore for Christmas and hooked up with her high school boyfriend, Duncan. She'd been lonely in Providence all fall and was hoping to get back together with Duncan, even if it had to be long-distance, since he went to Penn.

They made a date for New Year's Eve and ended up at a party where he talked to another girl all night. She felt melancholy on the train back to Providence, as if something she'd once counted on had been lost forever. In the back of her mind, she'd thought Duncan would always love her. But he didn't. Maybe he never had.

She'd barricaded herself in her room for the rest of the winter, reading poetry, living on Wheat Thins and Tab. Was she sad about Duncan? She wasn't sure. She just felt terrible.

"Wait a minute," Alyosha said. "I don't understand some of these things. What is Penn? What are Wheat Thins and Tab?"

She explained East Coast geography to him, the distances between Baltimore and Philadelphia, Baltimore and Providence. She told him that Wheat Thins were crackers and Tab was like Pepsi with fake sugar. He made a face at that but didn't question it.

"Then May came, and suddenly everything was better," she said. Partly because Josh had started hanging around. But she left that part out.

"So you have a sad love story in your past," he said. "I have one, too."

They walked along the embankment in front of the Hermitage, past the Field of Mars, and into a gated park. "The Summer Garden," he announced as they walked through the gate. "Have you been here before?"

"No, not yet."

"It's a good place." They strolled along the winding paths, which were shadowed by bare winter trees poking out of the snow. All along the paths stood giant wooden boxes like upright coffins.

"There are statues inside," Alyosha explained. "They cover them up for the winter. In the spring, the statues come back from the dead, emerging from their winter shrouds."

"Can we come back in the spring?" The park was crowded with the coffins, almost a hundred of them, and she wanted to see the statues.

"We will absolutely return in the spring," Alyosha promised. "It is a requirement of your Russian education." He paused in front of one of the boxes. "This one is special — my favorite as a boy. I will make a special point of showing it to you when we come back."

"What is it?"

"I can't tell you. I must show it to you. It's too soon to share such a thing, anyway."

"Share what?" She stared at the brown, snow-stained box and wondered what could be living inside it that meant so much to him, yet was too sensitive to talk about.

"Another poem has spontaneously erupted in my brain," he announced. "But if you are tired of poetry, I can suppress it."

"Don't suppress it. It's not healthy to suppress things," Laura said.

"This poem is by Anna Akhmatova and it is called 'Summer Garden.'"

Laura listened, straining to understand the unfamiliar words. She liked the last part the best:

. . . everything is mother-of-pearl and jasper,
But the light's source is a secret.

"My mother liked to bring me here in the summer," Alyosha said. "When I was older I sat on this bench and practiced drawing the statues. Once, I saw a man get arrested right there, near the fence."

"Who was it?"

"I don't know. He was young, but he had a long beard, which looked strange. His legs and arms twitched nervously, as if it took all his strength not to bolt out of the park. He restrained himself from running, but his eyes darted around in a panic. Suddenly three men in suits surrounded him. It was very subtle. They spoke quietly to the bearded man, and all three walked calmly out of the park and got into a car."

"Then what happened?"

"That was it."

"Did anyone say anything?"

"No one else seemed to notice that anything unusual had happened. Though maybe they were just pretending not to notice. Everyone here learns to pretend. If you notice what they're doing, they might come after you next."

In spite of the cold, they sat on a bench. Laura thought of the man who'd followed her off the tram and she shivered. This place was full of hidden dangers, and she hardly knew how to recognize them.

"Are you going to tell me your sad love story?" she asked.

"Maybe later."

She wondered who the star of that story was. Olga? Or maybe Tanya, the girl Olga hinted was a prostitute?

"What do you do when I don't see you?" Alyosha asked. "Have you made any friends?"

"Lots of new friends," she said. "Karen and Dan and all the other American students, and the Hungarians in the dorm, and some of the Soviet students . . ." She laughed. "Then there's my other roommate, Ninel. She's such a . . ." She slipped into English to find the right word. "A pill."

"A pill?" he echoed.

She tried another English word. "A drip?".

"Like water?" Alyosha asked, returning to Russian.

"She likes to follow all the rules, to the letter."

"Ah, a real Ninel. I always feel sorry for those girls named Ninel."

"Her brother is named Traktor."

Alyosha shook his head. "She has serious Communist Party parents. Either they really believe in the system, or they think giving their children patriotic names will protect them."

"Protect them? From what?"

"From trouble. Who ever heard of a traitor named Traktor?"

"I'd never heard of anybody named Traktor till now."

"Don't you have people named Lincoln and Washington?"

"Yes, but . . . that's different."

"Different how?"

"Lincoln and Washington were people, not farm machinery."

"And everyone in America has a gun. Right? Do you have a gun?"

"A gun? No! No one I know has a gun."

"That cannot be true. Statistically, there's at least one gun for every person in America."

"Maybe so, but in that case a few people are carrying the majority of the guns."

"So it is not true? Many Americans do not have guns?"

"Yes. No. It's not true."

Alyosha looked pained for a minute, but then he said, "I'm sure you are right. Here, television always gives the wrong idea about everything."

"Don't feel bad. Our TV is not so trustworthy, either."

He looked sad. "When I was little, I believed everything. I lived in the best city in the greatest country on Earth. My father was a captain in the greatest navy in the world. I went along with it all, the whole thing. I was a Young Pioneer, a Komsomol Youth leader, I wore my red kerchief. My parents were proud of me. . . ."

His voice trailed off. A seagull squawked from a floe of river ice.

"Then what happened?" Laura asked.

"My mother died. She went into the hospital for a routine surgery and got an infection there. It killed her."

"I'm sorry."

"Her doctor was incompetent, but my father refused to admit it. He can't admit anything is wrong with our system, with the government, with anything — ever." He touched his upper lip, as if it felt vulnerable. "I think he blamed my mother herself for dying. Like it was her fault. A heroic Soviet doctor could never make a mistake."

"How old were you when she died?"

"Fifteen. That's when I started drawing — I mean, seriously drawing. I'd always liked it, but I never thought of being an artist. My father denounced art as a waste of time. But after Mama died, the only thing that made me feel better was drawing. So I drew constantly. I did nothing but draw. I neglected my school-work, my friends, everything. . . ."

She touched his hand, glove on glove. He took off his glove and slipped his hand into hers. The two hands merged inside the warm cocoon.

"It was as if a veil fell from my eyes. Suddenly I saw every-thing differently. The hospitals are dirty, the stores are empty, the people are poor while the Party takes everything. The hypocrisy, the secrecy, the lies, the bullshit . . . I saw it all very clearly. I couldn't pretend to be a part of the system anymore. But that's what's required of you here — you don't have to believe the lies, but you must pretend you do. That's all that matters: the pretending. That's what keeps the whole system going."

"No one believes in it?" She touched a callous on his index finger, a rough bump.

"Maybe a few do. It doesn't matter. We don't get punished for what we believe; we're punished for what we say we believe. If people started telling the truth, what's really in their hearts and minds, the house would collapse. That's why dissidents are exiled or put in prison or into mental hospitals. If you dare to criticize the system, you must be crazy. You must be denounced. That belief is all that's holding this empire together."

The wind picked up and scraped Laura's cheeks. She knew all this. She'd heard it before. But she'd never met someone who'd been personally hurt by it before. And that made all the difference.

"Papa expected me to be an engineer, but I went to art school instead. After art school, the Artists Union would not accept me. They said my paintings were subversive, and consigned me to a menial job painting signs. Everyone must have a job of some kind, but we don't always get to choose what it is."

"Has your father seen your paintings?"

"Yes. He agreed with the Artists Union and called me decadent. He called me a parasite, a traitor. We had a big fight. He hasn't forgiven me or spoken to me since."

"So you've lost both of your parents."

"I understand how Papa feels. He lived through the war, starved in the siege, sacrificed everything for the good of his country. He has to believe in it. He can't allow himself to think it's all a sham. That would mean his life had been wasted."

"But what about you? You're his son. He's sacrificing you, too."

Alyosha smiled ruefully. "A small price to pay for the glory of the Motherland." His nose was red. He rubbed it. "You must be cold. Let's walk."

They left the park, keeping both hands inside her glove, and started for the Palace Bridge. Everything — the river, the bridge, the buildings, the snow — looked dreamy and half-formed, veiled by the dusk.

They paused at the bridge. She would cross the river, and he would go underground into the metro.

"I wish you could come back with me," he said.

"I do, too." She wished she could go anywhere but Dormitory Number Six. Someplace where she could be with him just a little bit longer.

"Call me soon." His hand still warmed hers inside the glove. She pressed her fingers against his.

"I will."

He pulled his hand out of the glove at last. She immediately felt its absence, cold air where his warm skin had been.

He put his hands, one gloved, one bare, on her shoulders, and bent his head toward hers. He kissed her, just a touch on the lips, but slowly, lingering there for a second longer than she thought he would. Then he raised his head, tilting it slightly to the left, and looked into her eyes as if searching for something.

His were brown, flecked with green and gold, and very sad.

He removed his hands from her shoulders with effort, as if resisting a great magnetic force. He turned and walked away to the metro. She stood on the edge of the bridge for a long time, watching him.

10

★

WOMEN'S DAY

heck it. Mail from home." Karen tossed a thin bundle of letters onto Laura's bed.

Laura flipped through the mail: three letters from her parents, two from her Brown roommate, Julie, one from her little brother, Sam, and one from Josh. She opened Josh's first.

Dear Laura,

I hope this letter reaches you before you leave. Right now I'm sitting in my apartment listening to reggae (Marley) and drinking Morning Thunder tea, even though it's 11 o'clock at night. I spent the day walking around trying to prove or refute a recent theory I formulated about women who wear very faded jeans. I think that they must screw like rabbits. I suspect women who wear dark jeans are repressed. So far I found two women who would seem to support the thesis and one who goes against it. I'll continue to collect the data until I reach a definitive conclusion.

Laura couldn't read further without pausing to mumble, "Ugh."

"I heard that." Karen was lying on her stomach, reading her own mail.

"Listen to this." Laura read Josh's letter out loud.

> *Laur, I really wish we could have continued the talk we started the night before you left. When your roommate showed up it broke the momentum, and when she finally went into her room I just couldn't continue — the talk wouldn't flow. So we never really settled anything —*
>
> *I've got to split for a few minutes, bye. —— Back again. Hello.*
>
> *Anyway, I don't feel like I know you well enough to promise anything, but I do want to say that I would like to see you when you get back to the States, and get to know you better. Maybe this is a stupid, not-well-thought-out response, but that's how I feel. So if you still like me in June, look me up. I'll be in Providence for the summer.*
>
> *I'm going to seal this up now and hope you read it before you leave Leningrad.*
>
> *Love, Josh, xo (I almost wrote ox instead of xo, but ox doesn't work for obvious semiological reasons)*

"Obvious semiological reasons?" Karen mocked. "Laura, you are not looking that guy up in June. I don't care if I have to go to Providence myself to stop you."

"He's smart," Laura said. "I mean, he's kind of intellectual."

"Yeah, his Theory of the Faded Jeans is absolutely brilliant."

Laura sighed. She saw it now. Josh wasn't an intellectual. He *posed* as an intellectual, spouting made-up theories and shallow opinions made to sound contrary and smart.

Alyosha didn't do that. He didn't have to. All he had to do to live a principled life was be himself. That act alone took courage. And he didn't expect anyone to applaud him for it. In fact, he was being punished for it.

"What are you thinking?" Karen asked.

"Nothing."

Providence seemed far away. It *was* far away. Josh was like a character in a movie she'd once seen, not a real person. Reality was this narrow bed she was lying on at that moment, with its thin, lumpy mattress. Karen, her friend, on the next bed, kicking her feet in thick hiking socks. The chipped wooden floor of their room. The tidy corner where Nina slept. Alyosha's hand inside her glove.

She was starting to like it here.

"Now for something completely different." She opened the first letter from her parents.

Dear Laurabear,

Honey, are you okay? Are you warm enough? How will we know for sure you're okay if there's no way to reach you??? Remember, if you have any health problems — anything at all — that constitutes an EMERGENCY and you must find a way to get whoever is in charge to allow you to CALL HOME. Do whatever it takes. We can't stand to think of you all alone over there and maybe SICK or DYING . . .

She read all three letters from her parents, which ran along the same lines, with weather reports and bits of news about her little brother's school exploits tossed in.

"Laurabear? Snort," Karen said.

"Okay, Miss Ohio. What's in your mail?"

Karen glanced at the letters spread out on her bed. "I got the usual crap from my parents about how being in the USSR is a unique opportunity and pay attention to everything. A letter from my roommate describing all the new bands she's into and all the great shows I'm missing, and one from Roy." She handed Roy's letter to Laura so she could see for herself. Roy was Karen's boyfriend from Oberlin, who was spending the semester abroad too — in Rome. "They're living in a villa or something, eating mind-blowing Italian food and guzzling wine."

Laura skimmed the details about the glories of fresh Parmesan cheese and real Italian pizza. Her stomach growled.

"It's not fair," she said.

"So not fair."

But, inexplicably, Laura was still happy to be in Leningrad.

"I have the whole day off on Monday," she told Alyosha on the phone the next time she called him. "For Women's Day."

"So do I," he said, though she had the impression that he pretty much worked whenever he felt like it. "Will you celebrate with me?"

"How do you celebrate Women's Day?"

"You'll see."

She had been lazy that day — it was snowing hard — and didn't bother walking the extra blocks to the farther-away phone booth. The man with the glasses was back, walking his dog in the blizzard.

She put it out of her mind.

"Happy Women's Day!" Nina had set flowers on the table and presented each of her roommates with a card. Laura opened hers. On the front was a painting of a red rose and the words MARCH 8. Inside it said, *Congratulations on Women's Day!* and it was signed, *Affectionately, Nina.* Karen got a similar card, and then Nina presented them with a box of chocolates to share.

"Thank you, Nina," Laura said. "Happy Women's Day to you, too."

She and Karen gave Nina a card and a box of Celestial Seasonings tea bags in assorted flavors.

Nina smiled and thanked them. She glowed happily as she bustled to the kitchen to make them all a pot of cinnamon tea. Everyone loved Women's Day. Or, anyway, the women did.

"I got you something, too," Karen said when Nina was out of the room. She gave Laura a handmade card, hastily drawn in pencil. On the front was a cartoon of Laura dressed like a babushka in an apron and head scarf. Inside, Karen had written, *Dear Comrade Laura: May I congratulate you on being a woman. Now get off your ass and shovel some snow! Love, Comrade Karen.*

"Very touching." Laura made a show of clutching the card to her heart. "Thank you, Comrade Karen."

"Natia invited me over for tea. Want to come? You'll like her."

"Can't. I'm going to Alyosha's."

"Shocker."

Maybe Laura was revolving her schedule around Alyosha, but she didn't care. There was no one she liked better. And Alyosha had a place all to himself — however he'd managed to get it — even if it was all the way on the outskirts of the city.

He opened the door holding a large bunch of blue flowers. "Mademoiselle." He kissed her hand. "I congratulate you on Women's Day."

"Thank you."

He stepped aside to let her in. The apartment was warm and smelled deliciously of butter and onions. He put her flowers in a vase and set them on the kitchen table.

"What are you making?" Laura asked.

"*Pelmenyi.* Have you ever tried them?"

"No." She'd heard of them but never tasted them.

"They're good. They'll be ready in a minute."

He sautéed some onions in butter while some kind of dumplings boiled in a pot on the stove. She sat and watched him. He wouldn't let her do anything to help, not even hand him a spatula.

"But I can't just sit here," she complained. "I feel useless."

"All right," he said. "Since you can't stand being waited on, you can give me an English lesson."

"Good. We'll speak English all through dinner." They were still speaking Russian.

"You'll tell me the words I don't know, though, right?" he said. "Because there will be many."

"I'll be your human dictionary. Starting . . . now."

Now that they were suddenly supposed to speak English, she didn't know what to say. She'd grown so used to speaking Russian with him that English felt unnatural. And that thought — along with the steam that filled the tiny kitchen when Alyosha drained the *pelmenyi* from the boiling pot — made her glow. Somehow along the way she'd become nearly fluent in Russian, even though she'd skipped a lot of language classes.

"Hey," she said in English. "I just realized my Russian's gotten pretty good."

He tossed the dumplings in the butter sauce. "Um . . . slower?"

Speaking English with him was not going to be so easy. "Dumplings. Mmmm." She smiled and rubbed her stomach, greedy with hunger.

He served her a plate of them drenched in butter. "Yes. Dumplings."

She sniffed the steam that rose from the plate, fragrant with butter and onions. "Butter."

He lifted the butter dish to show that he understood. Then he joined her at the table. She ate a dumpling. He waited for her reaction. "Tasty?" he asked in Russian.

She wagged a finger at him flirtatiously. "Uh-uh-uh. English only, please."

"Good?"

She ate another dumpling. They were slippery, with little meatballs inside. "Very good."

Slowly they ate. He watched with satisfaction as Laura finished all her *pelmenyi*. "Good job," he declared. "Now you are member of Lenin Clean Plate Club. Wait — I get your . . . prize? No. Wait. I bring."

He ran into the other room and soon returned with a star-shaped tin pin, enameled red, with a gold portrait in the center of Vladimir Lenin as a child. Underneath the portrait it said, *Lenin Clean Plate Club* in Russian. "From kindergarten. Age five." He pinned it to her sweater. She laughed.

"So the legends are true. There really is a Lenin Clean Plate Club."

"For real." He took a sip of beer. "I have idea."

"I have AN idea."

"I have an idea. You read me in English. English book. After dinner."

She liked the idea. "Which book?"

"You choose."

So, after dinner, he refused her pleas to help him clean up and sent her into the other room to pick out something to read. She studied his short shelf of English books: Hemingway, Kerouac, Shakespeare, Jack London, Dickens. The movie tie-in paperback of *The Great Gatsby* he had mentioned before. She pulled out *Great Expectations* and opened it to the first page.

"'My father's family name being Pirrup, and my Christian name Philip, my infant tongue could make of both names nothing longer or more explicit than Pip. So I called myself Pip, and came to be called Pip.'"

Alyosha wouldn't understand much of it, but the prose was so beautifully English. If he relaxed and let the words wash over him, he'd enjoy the sounds even if he didn't know what they meant.

He came into the room with tea, and they settled on the bed to read. He nodded happily at the book she'd chosen. "I read book in Russian. In school. So I know story of Pip."

"You need to work on your definite and indefinite articles," she teased. "The. I read THE book. I know THE story."

"You are THE bitch."

She laughed. "No, there you need an indefinite article. A bitch."

He leaned against the headboard with his mug of tea, unfazed. "Please to begin."

She cleared her throat and began to read. The words tumbled out of her mouth like cinnamon candies. He closed his eyes and listened.

"'Ours was the marsh country, down by the river, within, as the river wound, twenty miles of the sea. My first most vivid and broad impression of the identity of things seems to me to have been gained on a memorable raw afternoon towards evening.'"

She paused to turn the page. He bolted up as if she'd presented him with an opportunity that he must immediately seize.

"Laura."

She looked up from the book.

"I love you."

He put down his tea and took the book from her hands. She was too startled to resist. He leaned forward across the bed and kissed her. It was gentle, but she felt the urgency behind it. He would not stop kissing her unless she made him stop.

"*Liublyu tebya*," he whispered.

"English —"

"*Nyet.* English lesson is over."

She didn't want him to stop. She let herself fall back onto the bed and he followed, falling with her.

For the rest of the evening they spoke no more Russian, or English, but a language that they both understood completely.

11

THE FISHERMAN AND THE LITTLE GOLDEN FISH

She opened her eyes and found herself on the bed, on top of the blanket, in his arms. The radiator hissed. Her feet were cold. She didn't know how much time had passed, but the room was dark. Daylight had fled and blue night pressed against the bedroom window. Outside, a dog howled and a tram clanked by on the way to its last stop.

"Hey — what time is it?" Laura lifted her head and glanced around for a clock. Alyosha checked the alarm clock beside the bed and frowned. "Oh no." She sat up. It was almost midnight. "I missed the last train, didn't I?" She spoke in Russian. It was automatic now.

"You'll never make it in time." Alyosha nuzzled her neck. "So why not spend the night here?"

"I'll get in trouble. You don't understand. My room-mate Nina —"

"I know, she's one of those Ninels, little female Lenins. But what choice do you have?"

"Can I get a taxi or a car or something?"

"Not all the way out here. I'm so sorry, my Laura, my little fish. I'm afraid you are stuck. No use worrying about it." He brushed the hair off her forehead.

"But what if they kick me out of the program and send me home?"

"No one will know you are missing unless your roommate tells on you, right?"

"Right. But she's" — here her Russian failed her and she couldn't help slipping into English — "a total narc."

"What is *narc*?" As far as Alyosha was concerned, the time for English was over. He stuck to Russian.

"A tattletale."

"I know she seems like a slave to the system," Alyosha said. "But deep down she knows the system she defends is not real. She's just pretending."

"She seems pretty sincere to me."

"She's pretending *very hard*. We're all pretending. 'We pretend to work, and they pretend to pay us.'"

Laura had heard that old joke before.

"You never know. Perhaps Ninel likes you. Perhaps she won't turn you in. She just wants you to think that she will."

"Or maybe she's waiting for just the right moment. . . ."

Her back stiffened as she imagined the consequences of not

showing up for the night. But as he kissed her neck and ran a finger down her spine, she gradually relaxed until she found herself lying back on the bed, resigned to her fate.

"*Rebyonok* . . ."

"What does that mean?"

"'My little fish.' I don't know why, you seem like a pretty little fish to me. I could call you *kitten* or *little bird* or *tiny tiger*, but . . ." He studied her face, running a finger along her cheekbone. "I don't know why, but *little fish* just came to my lips. Maybe because your eyes are blue-gray like the sea."

She liked it, this Russian business of endearments and nicknames. "What should I call you?"

"Wait and see. Perhaps something will come to you." He leaned down to kiss her, and she thought of a tiger.

"I'm not sleepy," she said.

"Then let's get up."

He fixed them tea and sandwiches. They played all his Neil Young records late into the night. Laura explained the lyrics that Alyosha didn't understand, though she didn't understand all of them herself.

They finally got tired at three in the morning. He turned out the light and they lay in the darkness. Laura felt calm and relaxed. Nina and the dorm had vanished from her thoughts. Alyosha's eyes reflected the streetlight outside. They stared at the ceiling.

"Tell me a story," she said in Russian.

"Hmm . . . Okay." He turned on his side to face her, his arm draped over her ribs. "This is a story my mama used to tell me when I was little. Every Russian child knows it. It's an old folktale called 'The Fisherman and the Little Golden Fish.'"

Laura snuggled closer. It was warm under the covers but chilly outside. The tip of her nose felt cold. She warmed it against his shoulder.

"Once, a long time ago, there lived a poor old fisherman and his wife. They lived in a little tumbledown shack by the sea. The fisherman had been having very little luck. He cast his net into the ocean and pulled up nothing but mud. He threw the net again and came up with only seaweed. At last he tossed the net in one more time. This time he caught only one fish, but it was a golden fish such as he'd never seen before.

"'Put me back in the ocean, old man, and I'll give you whatever you wish,' the fish said. The fisherman was shocked. He'd lived by the sea all his life, but he'd never heard a fish talk before. He felt sorry as he watched the lovely fish squirm in the net, so he carefully untangled it, saying, 'Bless you, Golden Fish, but I don't want anything from you. Go back to your ocean realm and roam free.' The fisherman gently put the fish back into the ocean and he swam happily away."

A fairy tale. Laura sighed happily. Alyosha ran a finger along her forearm as he told the story.

"The fisherman went home and told his wife about the golden fish. 'He offered to grant me whatever I wished, but how could I ask for anything? I had to let him go.'

"'You fool!' cried the wife. 'You could have at least asked him for a new washtub. Ours is falling apart!'

"So the fisherman returned to the sea and called to the fish, 'Little golden fish, grant me a wish. . . .' The fish appeared in a blink and asked, 'What is it? What do you want?'

"The fisherman bowed. 'Forgive me, Your Majesty Golden Fish, but my wife wants a new washtub.'

"'Your wish has been granted. Go home and there you'll find a new washtub.'

"'Oh, thank you, kind fish!' cried the fisherman as the fish swam away.

"The fisherman ran home, and behold! There was a new washtub. But his wife wasn't happy. 'All you asked for is a washtub, when we could have had anything? You could have at least asked him for a new cottage. Look at this ramshackle dump we live in!'"

Laura laughed.

"So the fisherman went back to the seashore and called to the fish: *Little golden fish, grant me a wish.* . . . 'Forgive me, Your Majesty Golden Fish, but my wife won't stop scolding me, and now she wants a new cottage.'

"'It is done. Go home and see.'"

Laura yawned and grew sleepy as Alyosha went on, telling how the fisherman's greedy wife kept asking for more. First she wanted a cottage, then to be a fine lady in a mansion, and then to be a *czaritsa* in a palace, and the richer and grander she became, the meaner she was to her husband — except when she wanted him to ask the Golden Fish for more. *Little golden fish, grant me a wish. . . .*

By the time Alyosha finished the story, Laura was asleep. She didn't hear how it ended.

12

THE DOLL AND THE KEYS

A beam of sunlight lasered through a crack in the curtains. Alyosha kissed the spot where the light landed on Laura's cheek. "Happy Day-After-Women's-Day," he said.

He got up to open the curtain, and the room flooded with sun. She smiled and stretched. "I'm going to be so late for class." She wished she could stay there forever, nestled in that small apartment with Alyosha.

He got back under the covers with her. "Don't go."

"I have to. They take attendance. Anyway, don't you have to work?"

"Yes, but I move from one theater to the next, and no one is ever sure where I'm supposed to be at what time," he said. "And no one really cares, either. So I can pretty much do as I please. And what would please me right now is to make you breakfast."

He made tea and toast with gooseberry jam. He put the jam on his toast *and* in his tea, instead of sugar. "Try it, it's good."

127

She dipped a spoonful of jam into her tea and drank it. It immediately became a sweet berry tea, the most delicious tea she'd ever tasted.

"Oh! I forgot to give you your Women's Day gift yesterday." He went into the other room and returned with a small package wrapped in coarse gray paper. He'd decorated the paper with flowers drawn in blue pencil.

"You didn't have to do that." She touched the flowers.

"You might not like it. Open it."

Laura opened the package. Inside was a *matryoshka*, one of those nesting dolls that could be found in any Berioska Shop or souvenir stand. But this doll was not the usual smiling babushka in a head scarf. It was a close likeness of Laura. Laura as a *matryoshka* doll. Alyosha had painted her onto the doll, from her straight brown hair to her sheepskin coat and heavy rubber boots. Every detail was exactly right.

Laura opened her mouth. But she couldn't speak.

"There's more," Alyosha said. "Look inside."

She pulled off the top of the Laura doll. Nestled inside was a smaller doll, a little guy with brown eyes, brown hair, and a familiar blue parka that didn't look warm enough for winter. She gasped. It was Alyosha.

Alyosha bounced on his toes and rubbed his hands together. "Keep going . . ."

She pulled off the top of the Alyosha doll and there, resting at the bottom, were two keys on a Fiat keychain.

"What is this?"

"Keys to my apartment. So you can come over anytime. And if I'm at work or out shopping, you can just wait for me to come home."

She was stunned into silence. She didn't know what to say.

She tried to imagine Josh knowing her face and clothes so well he could paint a perfect likeness of her onto a doll from memory. She tried to imagine him giving her the keys to his apartment, telling her to come over anytime.

All she could see were his eyes like slits, smoking a joint, not meeting her gaze.

"You trust me with the keys to your apartment?"

He laughed. "Are you planning to rob me? There's nothing to steal!"

"No, but your —" She searched for the Russian word for *privacy*, but there wasn't one. She let the sentence hang unfinished.

"Privacy?" he said in English.

"Yes! You read my mind."

"I don't need *privacy* from you."

Maybe Olga wasn't such a threat after all.

"Thank you." She put the doll back together and leaned across the table for a kiss. "This is the most beautiful gift anyone has ever given me."

And it really was.

★

She had an essay due for Grammar class that day. She scribbled it on the metro while she rode from Avtovo to school.

Family Traditions and Holidays in America
By Laura Reid

I recently enjoyed my first celebration of International Women's Day. My hand is practically black and blue from being kissed all day. I wish we had this holiday in America. The closest thing we have is probably Valentine's Day. On Valentine's Day boys and girls give cards and chocolates to each other. It's fun in elementary school but when you get older somehow it always turns out to be a big disappointment. American boys almost never kiss your hand. And they have no idea how to behave on Valentine's Day. Instead of giving delightful cards and gifts, most of them shrug and say things like "I don't like holidays" or "Valentine's Day is just a corporate plot to sell greeting cards" or "It's not my thing." That leaves it up to the girls — one's friends, sisters, mother — to make Valentine's Day festive by engaging in the ritual of mass gorging on candy. It's nice to get a card from your mother, I suppose, but it doesn't exactly set your heart racing.

My first year of college, my roommate bought a big jar and filled it with chocolate hearts and jelly beans for Valentine's Day. She and I and our girlfriends across the hall kept reaching into the jar for candy and saying, "I can't stop eating this candy! Someone stop me!" Finally, a boy who was studying math with my roommate got fed up. He said, "Let me help you girls out," and then he picked up the big jar of candy and dumped it all out the window. "No!!!" we all screamed. "Why did you do that?"

"You said you wanted to stop eating it," the cruel boy said. "So I stopped you. Now we can get back to studying math."

I ask you, is that any way to celebrate a holiday about love and sugar? Would a Russian man throw his women friends' candy out the window on Women's Day? I highly doubt it. Unless he was drunk.

The End.

She didn't have time to proofread it before she turned it in. She'd missed Translation and was five minutes late for Grammar as it was.

Karen looked up with relief as she slipped into the classroom and took the seat next to her. Galina Petrovna, their Grammar professor, didn't look so pleased.

"Laura Reid, you missed class on Friday and now you're late. Do you realize that your grade depends on attendance, promptness, and participation?"

"I'm sorry, Galina Petrovna. I'll try to do better."

"Have you done the homework?" Galina Petrovna glared at her as if she expected the answer to be no. Her expression didn't soften when Laura tore three scribbled pages from her notebook and turned them in.

Karen wrote *We're back in high school* in her notebook and tilted it so Laura could see.

"You lose a grade for sloppiness," the instructor continued. "And that's just to start." She dropped the pages on her desk. "We're going over the exercises on page thirty-five of the text. Continue, Maureen Binkowski."

Binky read the lesson on verbs of motion. Karen scribbled another note. *Where the f were you all night?*

Laura wrote back, *Later.*

"You lucked out." Karen pushed a tray along the cafeteria counter, sighing at the unappetizing lunch food: a blob of gristly meat, milk soup with scraps of bread in it, and cabbage. "Nina came back from a Women's Day party a little tipsy and passed out early. I mussed up your bed before she woke up this morning so she'd think you slept in it last night."

"You're the best." Laura took a roll and a glass of milky coffee.

"Then I told her you left early for class. Like that would ever happen." Karen reached for a coffee and looked hard at Laura's face. "You are blissed out."

Laura nodded at a table in the corner of the cafeteria and they sat down. "He said he loved me."

"Alyosha?"

"Of course Alyosha."

"And — ?"

"I think I love him too," Laura said.

"Laura, no . . ."

"Why not? He's wonderful!"

"Yeah, he's great, but are you sure you can trust him? He's got a huge ulterior motive."

"It's not like that."

"You're not the only one who thinks she's in love. Some ballerina's got Dan wrapped around her bony little finger, Clara has fallen for a dissident folk singer, and Mark Calletti, world's biggest geek, is in love with three different girls. And some guy proposed to me on the street the other day."

"So?"

"So, don't you think it's a little suspicious that we are so irresistible to Russians? That within a couple of months half the group is practically engaged? Remember what Stein and Durant told us at orientation?"

Laura hesitated. She remembered, and it wasn't as if she hadn't thought about this before. Many Russians were eager to leave the Soviet Union, and the easiest way out was marriage to a foreigner. She knew.

But then she remembered Alyosha on the bed, listening to her read, and then not listening to her read. . . .

The night she'd spent with him did not feel like a lie.

"Laura?"

"Okay, it's a little suspicious. For everybody else. Alyosha is different."

"Laura, come on. Keep your head. You know what's happening here."

"It's more complicated than that," Laura insisted.

"It always is."

"He hasn't asked me to marry him —"

"— yet —"

"— and I'm not planning on marrying anyone. But how can I make friends with anyone here if I'm always suspicious of their motives?"

Karen sighed, releasing a little steam from her argument. "You can't, I guess. But, listen — you can't stay over at his place all night anymore. You got lucky this time, but next time Nina's going to report you, and you don't know what will happen then. You could get kicked out, or maybe they'll just put somebody on your tail. They'll find Alyosha, and he's the one who'll pay the price."

A sobering thought. She imagined a man in a suit knocking on Alyosha's door, going through all his Western treasures, his books, his records, his clothes — just having those things was enough to make him suspect — and taking him away somewhere, never to be heard from again. Like the man Alyosha saw as a boy, arrested in the Summer Garden. His life ruined.

She didn't want to be responsible for ruining anyone's life.

"I'll be careful," she promised. "From now on."

13

★

DOSTOYEVSKY'S HOUSE

*T*his was how she knew she loved Alyosha: She never found herself weighing his good qualities versus the bad qualities — his sexy wide mouth, his milky skin, the roundness of his fingertips and the firm yet gentle way they gripped her hand, versus . . . what? She couldn't come up with anything bad. If it was a part of him, she loved it. But that wasn't the point. She didn't love his good qualities. She loved *him*. Just him. All of him.

And she sensed that he felt the same way about her. That he wasn't judging her the way Josh did — did she look hot that day? Was she nagging him? Had she said something funny? Was she getting on his nerves? Alyosha didn't seem to think that way. He just liked her.

Loved her. That's what he'd said. He loved her.

That made her love him even more.

If only she could see him all the time. But she had to go to class, had to sleep in the dorm, had to live her student life most of the time. She wandered around the city as the ice began to thaw and tried to remember how it had looked to her when she first arrived. Dingy, dreary, lifeless . . . Leningrad had seemed like the most unromantic place on earth. Even the name — *Leningrad* — sounded utilitarian, unromantic.

But now the city had been transformed. Nothing bloomed yet; it was early spring, the mounds of dirty snow were shrinking, the ice on the Neva was breaking up and floating out to sea, but the trees showed only the slightest sign of budding, and people still waddled down the streets in their heavy coats and felt boots.

No, it wasn't spring that had transformed the city, but something else — her own eyes. Where once they'd seen decay, waste, and grim gray skies, they now saw beauty, history, and a moody atmosphere, a sense of mystery. The palace walls of eggshell blue and butter yellow, the gleaming golden domes of old churches, the mesmerizing classical pattern on the gate of the Summer Garden, the statues of horses and men that seemed to come alive in the dusk, the fog drifting off a winding canal, a melancholy glance between two girls her age . . . To her this was no longer Leningrad. It was St. Petersburg.

Yes. That had a nicer ring to it.

St. Petersburg. *The most romantic city in the world* . . . she thought as she passed the Sailors Monument on the University Embankment, the statue of Peter and his horse, ready to jump off the rock they were perched on, the winding canals adorned with statues, the house where the poet Pushkin had lived, the narrow streets Dostoyevsky had paced, courting madness. It was all beautiful, and she wanted to walk the streets for hours, do nothing but look at everything and dream, when she wasn't with Alyosha.

But of course, she hadn't come to Leningrad to dream. She was supposed to go to class, to read and study, to write papers and learn the difference between transitive and intransitive verbs.

She couldn't do it. She couldn't read, couldn't do her home-work, couldn't concentrate, could barely manage a coherent conversation. All she could do was wait for bedtime to come so she'd finally be free to lie in the dark and dream about Alyosha.

The next time they met, Alyosha took her to Fyodor Dostoyevsky's apartment, now a museum, on Kuznechnyi Lane. "This is where he lived after he was released from prison in Siberia," Alyosha told her. "It's where he wrote *The Brothers Karamazov*, and where he died."

The apartment was dark and gloomy. Laura tried to picture the great writer sitting at the massive desk, scribbling novels by candlelight on the long winter nights, remembering — or try-ing to forget? — the horrors of Siberia.

They looked at his books, at the notes he wrote to his daugh-ter and left on the dining-room table, at the cigarettes he had rolled, ready to be smoked.

They left the museum and started down the lane. Alyosha took her hand. "Want to see Raskolnikov's house?"

"You mean it's a real place? But he's a fictional character. . . ."

"Yes, but all the settings in *Crime and Punishment* are real. The police station, Sonia's house, the pawnbroker's house —"

Laura shuddered. Raskolnikov, the hero of *Crime and Punishment*, killed an old woman pawnbroker just to see if he could, to prove he was a superior man. He didn't get away with it, of course — that was the Punishment part of the story.

Raskolnikov's house was a nondescript apartment building on Grazhdanskaya Street. They went inside and up the dark stairwell. "Raskolnikov lived in an attic garret," Alyosha whispered. The walls of the stairwell were covered with graffiti: *Raskolnikov lives in each of us. Raskolnikov, kill my neighbor. Raskolnikov was here.*

"This is what I came for," she whispered so softly she wasn't sure if Alyosha heard her. Here was the Russia she'd loved since childhood, the dark, violent, passionate place where the life of the mind and spirit were as real as the life of the body. She'd found it at last. She squeezed Alyosha's hand in the dark.

The garret door was closed and locked — someone lived there now. Laura touched the wood. Beyond that door had once lived a tortured soul. He was fictional, but he felt real.

"Should we knock?" Alyosha asked.

Laura shook her head. "I couldn't bear to see some . . . I don't know, office worker or something . . . living in Raskolnikov's garret."

"Some low-level Party functionary," Alyosha teased.

"Or the reporter who covers ice hockey for *Pravda.*"

They laughed quietly. Back outside, it was snowing. They continued the tour, passing the murdered pawnbroker's house, which somehow rattled with horror even though it looked ordinary enough, and the canal-side building where Sonia, the saintly prostitute who redeemed Raskolnikov's soul, was supposed to have lived.

"Are you cold?" Alyosha asked. "Let's go somewhere and warm up."

They went to a café. It was bustling and crowded. As they wove their way through the packed tables, Laura spotted a familiar curly head in the corner: Dan.

"There's one of my friends," she told Alyosha, pulling him by the hand.

Dan was sitting with a fine-boned girl, black haired, pale-skinned, with birdlike hands. "Laura!" he exclaimed when he saw her. "Sit with us."

Speaking Russian as a courtesy to Dan's friend, Laura introduced Alyosha, and Dan introduced the girl he was with as Lena. "She's a dancer with the Kirov."

"In the corps," she said modestly, but her tone was not modest at all. She and Alyosha eyed each other warily as he and Laura sat down.

"Alyosha's a painter," Laura said.

"Oh? Are you a member of the Artists Union?" Lena asked.

Alyosha shifted uncomfortably in his seat. "No."

"We're sharing a bottle of champagne." Dan snatched the bottle from its ice bucket. "Or what passes for champagne around here. Want some?"

"Sure," Laura said.

"I'll have tea," Alyosha said.

Dan signaled for a waiter, who ignored him. "Legendary Soviet service," he joked. When the waiter came at last, he ordered tea for Alyosha and two extra champagne glasses "in case you change your mind."

"How can you say you're an artist if you're not an official member of the union?" Lena pressed.

"I make art," Alyosha said. "Isn't that the definition of an artist?"

"Yes, but any child can draw a picture," Lena said. "That doesn't necessarily make him an artist."

"Alyosha's work is beautiful." Laura couldn't understand why there was so much tension between them, when, as far as she knew, they'd never met before.

"I'd love to see it sometime," Dan said. "Where have you been all day, Laura? I didn't see you in class this afternoon."

"We went to the Dostoyevsky museum. Did Raisa Ivanovna notice I was gone?"

"Of course she noticed. If you're not careful, you're going to fail Translation."

Laura gave a happy shrug. She couldn't care less about anything in the world than she did about Translation class.

"Lena's dancing in *Giselle* tonight," Dan said. "Want to come? I can get a couple more tickets — right, Lena?"

Lena's nod was cold, the slightest tilt of the head. Laura glanced at Alyosha, who said, "Thanks, but not tonight."

Laura gave Dan an apologetic look; she could tell he was as baffled by the Russians' behavior as she was. "Maybe another night."

"Anytime. Just let me know."

Alyosha plucked at her sleeve. "We should go."

"But you haven't had your tea yet."

Alyosha rose. "I don't want tea. Let's go."

"All right." Laura stole a sip of Dan's champagne, then stood up to leave. "Nice to meet you, Lena. See you back at Number Six, Dan."

Alyosha was already halfway out of the café when she caught up to him. "What was that all about? Why were you in such a hurry to leave?"

"I didn't like that girl."

"I don't think she liked you, either. But why?"

"She's . . . a certain type. You can't trust that kind of girl. Ask Olga about it."

"Olga?" She remembered what Olga had said about Alyosha's old girlfriend, Tanya. How she hung around foreigners' hotels, which was supposed to mean she was some kind of prostitute, or the next thing to it.

"She knew I knew what she's up to. That's why she was unfriendly."

"What is she up to?"

They were walking so fast — she struggled to keep up with Alyosha's pace — that they'd already reached the metro station.

"What are we doing now? Are you going home?" *Am I coming with you?* she added to herself. She really shouldn't; she had classes in the morning, and she'd surely get into trouble if she didn't come home yet again. But she wanted to go with him. She wanted to solve this riddle, make things happy again between them. She wouldn't be able to rest if they left things like this and she didn't understand why he was angry.

"Look: You don't understand. You can't understand. So just forget about it."

He started down the metro stairs.

"Alyosha, wait!" She chased after him, grabbed his sleeve. He stopped and whirled around. His face flashed with anger, but it softened as soon as he took in her pleading eyes.

"Laura." He put his arms around her. Rush hour commuters shoved and elbowed them on their way to the metro. "I'm sorry."

She was close to tears. "I'm so confused. You're right — I don't understand. Why won't you explain it to me?"

"Okay. I'll try." He kissed her forehead. "I don't like for you to meet people like Lena, because I don't want you to think all Russians are like her. Some are — maybe even a lot — but not all."

"Like her how?" Laura asked.

"Dishonest." He frowned. "Greedy. Willing to use people to get what they want."

"How do you know Lena is like that?"

"It's in her attitude, her posture. The way she looks at your friend Dan. Whatever is between them, it isn't love. I can see it. Any Russian could see it. Americans don't seem to recognize this look so well. Maybe they are used to falseness, I don't know. Maybe they like it. . . ."

Now that he'd drawn her attention to it, Laura could see what he meant about Lena, her haughty attitude hiding a desperate unhappiness. Lena imagined she belonged somewhere else, in the glamorous West, where she'd live as she was meant to in a fine house and beautiful clothes, a dancer on an international stage. If Dan could take her to that wonderful world, what did it matter whether she loved him or not? The most important thing was to get to that place where she belonged, however she could.

"We don't like falseness," she said. "Not all of us, anyway. I feel the same way you do. I don't want you to think that all

Americans are like Dan. He knows Lena is using him, so he is using her right back. You're right, that isn't love."

He put his arms around her. "I know you aren't like Dan."

"I know you're not like Lena. They have nothing to do with us. We have to stop thinking of ourselves as Russian and American. We're just Alyosha and Laura."

"If you were Russian, I'd love you just the same," he said. "You could be Chinese, Indonesian, Kenyan, Peruvian . . . it wouldn't change anything."

He kissed her again, on the lips this time, and she believed him. A babushka loudly clucked her tongue at them and smacked Laura's leg with a string bag full of onions. Laura felt her leg buckle but ignored it, giving all her attention to her lips.

He released her and looked at her tenderly, still holding her close. "I heard what your friend Dan said: You must go to class. I'll go home alone tonight and think of you."

"When will I see you again?" *Tomorrow*, she thought. *I want to see you tomorrow.*

"Call me tomorrow."

One more kiss, and he turned and joined the stream of people flowing toward the metro. She watched the escalator carry him deep under the ground and far away from her.

14

★

SURPRISE

*P*honetics is the best," Karen said as they left Semyon Mikhailovich's class Friday afternoon. She stopped short, adding, "There's a sentence I never imagined myself saying."

It was Laura's favorite class, too. That day they'd read Anna Akhmatova's poem "The Summer Garden." Their assignment was to memorize it by next week. Laura had already memorized it. She had her own poignant memories of the Summer Garden, and it made her miss him.

"I'm going to go call Alyosha," she told Karen.

Karen laughed. "Didn't you just see him yesterday? Dan said his ballerina friend didn't like him."

"Yeah. That was weird."

"You're getting attached to him, aren't you? What are you going to do when we go to Moscow tomorrow night?"

"That's tomorrow night?" She'd almost forgotten about their spring-break trip to Moscow. Everyone was looking forward to the break from classes and the change of scenery. And staying in hotels instead of the crappy dorm. But a week away from Alyosha . . . She counted how many weeks were left in the semester. Eight weeks. Not many.

Eight weeks until she had to leave him forever.

Now she really needed to see him. She'd explain about the trip, how she wouldn't have another chance to see him before she left. She dropped Karen at the dorm and walked to her special phone booth. The man with the dog wasn't around. She dialed Alyosha's number, but there was no answer.

He was probably at work.

Then she remembered: his keys. She had his keys.

She could go to his apartment and wait for him. Surprise him. She could even have dinner ready for him.

He wanted her to. That was why he gave her the keys.

She trotted back to the dorm, excited about her plan. Nina was in the kitchen with her friend Alla. Karen was sitting at the table in their room, doing homework. She looked up when Laura bounced in.

"What are you so happy about?" Karen asked.

"I'm going to see Alyosha."

"For a change. Don't forget to come home before midnight."

"I'll try not to."

She changed into fresh clothes; took the keys from their hiding place within the Laura/Alyosha doll, which was hidden in one of her socks in her armoire; and set off for Avtovo.

★

She arrived at his door loaded down with a bundle of food. She'd found a stand selling oranges near the metro station, and the line wasn't even that long, so she bought as many as she could get. She stopped for bread and cheese and a bottle of kvass. She was getting the hang of this Soviet shopping thing.

She put down her bag in the hallway outside his apartment and fumbled in her coat pocket for his keys. She found them and paused. She thought she heard a noise, a thump, through the door. He must have come home. She jangled the keys in her hand, then decided to knock.

She waited for him to throw the door open, cry "Laura!" and pull her inside with a bear hug. But he didn't. Nothing happened.

She knocked again and listened at the door. She thought she heard another thump, couldn't be sure . . . but no one answered her knock.

Could someone have broken in? Was there a robber inside? Did they even have robbers in the Soviet Union?

Or what if it was the secret police, searching his place? The KGB?

The apartment was quiet. She put the key in the lock and turned it.

She opened the door and stepped inside. "Hello?"
Nothing.

Not bothering to take off her wet boots, she took two steps down the hall and peered into the living room, terrified of what she might find.

"Laura! What are you doing here?"

Olga was stretched out on the bed, a notebook open in front of her. From where she stood in the doorway, Laura could see sketches and scribbles in Alyosha's blocky handwriting. Olga was barefoot and wet-haired, wearing one of Alyosha's long shirts, a throw blanket tossed over her legs.

"Didn't you hear me knock?" Laura asked.

"I thought it was a neighbor, so I didn't bother to answer. I wasn't expecting you!"

Obviously. "I came over to make dinner for Alyosha. What are you doing here, Olga?"

Olga sat up and shut the notebook she'd been reading. She pulled the blanket around her shoulders. "I come over here sometimes to get away from Roma," she confessed. "We live with two other families. There's no place to be alone in our apartment, and Lyosha has this whole place to himself."

This explanation didn't seem like enough, somehow. "But how did you get in?"

Olga waved her hand dismissively at the doorway. "I picked the lock. That lock is worthless."

"Oh." Laura let her bag of groceries sink to the floor. "Do you do this a lot?"

"When I can get away."

"Where is Alyosha?"

"I don't know."

"But if you don't know where he is, how do you know he won't come home and find you here?"

Olga shrugged. "If he finds me, he finds me. He won't mind. We're old friends." A sly smile tainted Olga's pretty face.

"Maybe I should go —"

"What?" Olga jumped up. "No. Stay, Laura. We can talk together until Lyosha comes home. Girl talk."

Girl talk wasn't what Laura had pictured when she'd planned the evening.

"No, I've got to get back. I can't stay out late anyway."

"That's right, you live in a dormitory. You have rules to follow. Oh well. I'll just stay here until Lyosha comes back. I'll tell him you stopped by —"

"Um, okay." Laura left the groceries on the floor and fled. She ducked her head against a brisk spring wind as she walked to the metro. The cold air stung her eyes, made them water. She reached the metro station, descended, and tried not to think of what was happening back at the apartment without her.

The next morning Laura hopped the tram to school, running late and in no mood to face the gypsies on the bridge, even if they did avoid her now. The day was frosty and gray, and so were the faces around her. The tram was crowded. A little girl clutched her mother with one hand and a blue balloon with the other. A scruffy man with wild, haunted eyes and bits of egg yolk in his beard stared at Laura as if she were the devil. Just as she was about to get off the tram, he leaned close and whispered, "Beware." At that moment, the little girl's balloon popped.

Laura jumped, her nerves rattled. The bearded man followed her off the tram. She ran through the university gates, and he kept going down the embankment toward the choppy water, mist rising off the ice.

She'd hardly slept the night before, imagining Alyosha coming home to find Olga wearing his shirt and . . . what then? Wasn't Olga married? She sure didn't act like it.

Laura could call Alyosha and ask him what had happened. But would he tell her the truth?

She didn't know. She didn't want to risk getting the wrong answer.

Maybe she'd never call him again.

Still she thought about him every minute, every second. He might have an explanation for Olga's behavior. Maybe he hadn't slept with Olga after Laura left. Maybe he'd asked her to leave. If he really wanted Olga hanging out in his apartment, he could have given *her* keys.

Maybe Olga didn't want to sleep with him.

Laura laughed. Obviously she did want to.

She dazed through her classes. Her Composition teacher returned her Women's Day essay, dripping in red pencil and graded a 3, the equivalent of a C. Laura had never received a C in a non-math class in her life. At one time, getting a C on an essay would have hurt. But she felt nothing. She didn't care about school, didn't care about grades, didn't care what her teachers thought of her.

Russia was working its black magic on her spirit. For good and for ill.

She didn't wait for Karen after classes ended. She trudged across campus to the Builders' Bridge to pack for the trip to Moscow.

As she approached the arc of the bridge, she saw someone standing there, right in the middle, blocking the way. A young man.

She walked closer and knew just from the way he hunched against the wind, his hands in his pockets, that it was Alyosha. The gypsy women fluttered nearby like nervous birds.

Without thinking, without knowing what she was doing, she ran to him and flung herself into his arms. He held her close, pressed his lips to her cheek.

"Why didn't you call me?" he asked.

"I was mad. I'm sorry."

"Because of Olga?" He took her hand and they walked over the bridge toward the dorm. "She's crazy. Pay no attention to her."

"But . . . I think she loves you." ,

"So? I don't love her. She comes over to make Roma jealous. He came and got her soon after I got home. I made dinner for all three of us out of the delicious things you brought and wished for you to call."

She felt terrible for leaving him hanging like that, when he had no way of reaching her. No way but this: showing up and finding her. Which was risky for both of them, so close to the university. Her professors or chaperones might see them and demand to know who he was. . . . They might tell her to stop seeing him, or they might look into his background, or bring him in for questioning. She didn't really know what could happen, and it was hard for her to imagine, but there was an air of danger when she was with him.

He put his arm around her as they walked, in spite of the risk. "Tomorrow is Saturday. Let's do something together. Maybe go to a concert. If I tell the box office I'm a tour guide and you're my guest, we could get great seats —"

"I can't." She could hardly look at him.

"Why not?"

"I'm going away tonight. We're all going away. The American students. To Moscow."

He stopped, his expression tightening, and removed his arm from her shoulder. "I don't understand. What do you mean, you are going away?"

"It's our spring vacation. Our chaperones are taking us on a trip."

"For how long?"

"A week."

"But you can't leave. I can't live without you for a week."

"I have to go. I have no choice."

The look on his face nearly broke her heart. The tightness around his mouth melted into sadness, and his brown eyes seemed to search the air around her, looking for a safe place to land.

"I'm afraid something will happen to you if you go away from me for so long," he confessed.

"What do you mean? Nothing will happen to me —"

"I mean, you will fall out of love with me. You'll fall for someone else — one of your American boys, perhaps. Like Dan."

"Dan? We're friends, that's all." She couldn't resist adding a tiny jab. "Like you and Olga."

"That's exactly what I mean! People can be treacherous. I don't want to lose you."

"You won't lose me."

"Someone might try to talk you out of seeing me. Your chaperones, maybe."

"They can't talk me out of anything. Besides, they don't know about you."

Two young men strolled by, and Alyosha took half a step away from her. He waited until they passed, and then studied them as they walked away. "Don't let your chaperones know."

"I won't. I promise. But we'll be back, and you and I can do anything you like." And by then — she couldn't help calculating — how much time would she have left? Seven weeks.

"We see each other so little," he said. "Every moment is precious to me."

"To me, too." She watched his sad eyes, trying to get them to settle on hers, to reassure him. She couldn't make him feel better if he wouldn't look at her.

"Then don't go away."

"Alyosha, I have to."

"All right. I must accept this, I suppose."

They started walking again. She told him a little about her itinerary, so he could imagine her there while she was away. "We're staying at the Hotel Rossiya — have you ever been there? It supposed to be the biggest hotel in the world."

He'd never stayed there, though he'd seen it the last time he visited Red Square, on a school trip. They walked past Dormitory Number Six without pausing. They knew they couldn't be spotted near there. A few blocks away, they stood in the gated doorway of an old house. Alyosha pressed his back against the gate and pulled her to him. "*Rebyonok . . .*"

They kissed in the doorway. The day was dying. Laura had to pack for the trip and get ready to leave on the midnight train.

"I have to go," she said. "I'll miss you."

"I will wilt without you."

"I'll call you as soon as we get back. It's only one week."

"One endless week."

She walked back to the dorm alone, just to be safe, in case Ivan the guard happened to be looking out the window. He might notice Laura and a strange Russian boy walking down the street at the same time and call it a coincidence; but if he saw them coming back together, he'd know that wasn't by chance. She could feel Alyosha a few yards behind her, following her down the street like a guardian angel. She didn't dare turn around and look. She didn't have to. His presence was tangible. When she reached the front door of the dorm, she paused. He strolled by as if he had nothing to do with her, but she saw his quiet smile, the sparkle in his eye.

15

★

MIDNIGHT TRAIN TO MOSCOW

*A*t ten P.M. the American students and their chaperones, Dr. Stein and Dr. Durant, boarded the midnight train to Moscow. Laura and Karen shared a sleeping compartment with Binky, and Dan sneaked in with them.

Dan whipped out a bottle of pale yellow vodka and rubbed his hands together. "Party time! We drink, we pass out, we wake up in Moscow."

"What *is* that stuff?" Karen asked.

"Bison Piss," Dan said. "I got it special at the Berioska. It's flavored with buffalo grass, or something, that grows in Poland." He produced a stack of short paper cups and poured out shots for all of them.

Binky stared dubiously into her cup. "Looks like a urine specimen."

"Don't look at it — drink it. *Na zdorovye.*"

They tossed back the vodka. Dan grunted, *"Akh!"* Russian style.

"You've really gone native," Laura said.

"Same to you," Dan said. "How's Alyosha?"

"Fine." Just hearing his name gave her heart a jolt. "How's Lena?"

"A bitch. As you saw. But she's pretty."

"Why was she so snooty to Alyosha?"

Dan shrugged. "They're both after the same thing. And they don't want other Russians sniffing around and spoiling their game."

Laura bristled.

"What are you talking about?" Binky asked.

"Lena's looking for a ticket out of here," Dan explained. "So's Alyosha. But they don't want us — their tickets — to see how valuable we are. How many people want us. They don't want us to realize that they're using us. They want us to think they're in love with us, that it's real, the one and only thing."

"Alyosha's not using me," Laura said.

Dan laughed. "Good one." On Laura's hurt look, he changed his expression. "I mean, come on. You know how it works here."

"Can I have some more vodka?" Binky asked.

"You like to think she's using you because then it gives you a free pass to use her," Laura shot back. "It's just a game to you. Not love. A game. And if that's what you want to do, that's fine.

But don't you dare say that's what's happening with me and Alyosha. You're not there. You don't see."

Dan passed her the bottle without looking at her. "Laura, I'm sorry. I didn't mean he doesn't care about you —"

Laura passed the bottle to Binky without drinking. When she was with Alyosha, she had no doubts about him. It was when she was away from him that the doubts crept in.

The trip would be a test. A test of her faith, her feelings, her resolve. She would return to Leningrad with her doubts about Alyosha growing — or more in love with him than ever.

Maybe that was why Alyosha didn't want her to go away. He didn't want her feelings tested, in case they didn't pass.

Mark Calletti knocked on the door. "Hey. Who's got the vodka?"

Soon there was a full-on party raging in Laura's compartment. The train jolted, lurched, and chugged slowly out of the station. By morning they'd be in Moscow.

She woke up at sunrise and peeked out the window. The train rolled through the snow-covered countryside, past birch forests and tiny wooden villages out of a fairy tale.

She put on her coat and slipped into her boots for the walk down the chilly corridor to the bathroom. At the end of the car, a babushka busied herself with a tea cart. She sold tea and rolls for a few kopeks each. On her way back to her compartment, Laura bought four rolls and a pot of tea.

Outside, the scenery was quickly shifting from villages to small cities, factories, desolate apartment buildings, a smoky sky, grimy streets. They were getting close to Moscow.

The grand avenues of Moscow rolled by through the steamed-up bus window while Irina, their Intourist guide, lectured them on the sights. Laura was glad she was spending the semester in Leningrad; Moscow was ugly. As they neared their hotel, the medieval spires of St. Basil's Cathedral rose over Red Square, striped, multicolored domes that looked as if they were made out of Play-Doh, the glorious monument to Ivan the Terrible and the dark and bloody history of Russia.

At the Hotel Rossiya — a massive rectangle built in the 1960s in the Soviet Modern style, sterile and ugly but conveniently located next to Red Square — she and Karen roomed with Binky. They picked up their keys from the cranky woman who guarded their floor from a desk at the end of the hall. She kept all the keys, and hotel guests had to stop at her desk whenever they came or went from the hotel. She also had a samovar for tea.

"Because it's inhuman to ask a person to go more than an hour without tea," Karen said.

"Just one more way for them to keep track of us," Binky said.

After a hotel breakfast they met their guide, Irina, for a tour of the Kremlin. Hundreds of people were lined up around Red Square to see the corpse of Lenin in Lenin's tomb. Irina led them past the armed guards straight to the front of the line — the usual special treatment.

"Vladimir Ilich Lenin died in 1924," Irina lectured as they stared at the bald, goateed, waxy corpse lying on a bed of red silk and encased in crystal.

"He looks like an exhibit at Madame Tussauds," Binky whispered, but all Laura could think of, strangely, was Snow White lying on her crystal bier after she eats the poison apple, before the prince kisses her back to life.

"They've kept this corpse together for almost sixty years," Dan said.

"Jesus," Karen mumbled.

"When do we get to go to the Berioska?" Binky whined. "I heard the Moscow shops have stuff you don't see in Leningrad."

"I'm dying for a bite of Jarlsberg cheese," Karen said. "Just one bite."

That night, Laura went with Dan and Karen to the Marine Bar at the US Embassy. It was Dan's idea. The sight of US Marines — armed, on duty, guarding the American Embassy — was a bit of a shock. The marines, crisp and shorn in red, white, and blue, looked healthy, rich, and clean.

The Marine Bar was crowded. It was movie night, and they were showing *Take This Job and Shove It*. The room was decorated to look like a roadhouse, with American movie posters and pennants from American sports teams strung along the walls.

Country music played on the sound system as Laura and her friends settled at a picnic table, ready to devour some hamburgers, milk shakes, and Budweiser.

"I don't even like Bud." Karen plinked her beer can with her fingernail. "But this does taste refreshing."

Laura's chocolate milk shake arrived while they waited for their burgers and fries. She took a sip.

"How is it?" Karen asked. Laura had been looking forward to a milk shake for weeks. Her stomach was primed. But she made a face.

"Disappointing. Not chocolatey enough." She took another sip. "And it has that weird Russian-ice-cream taste. I don't know what it is, but it's not right." *It tastes like cream*, she remembered Alyosha saying. She took one last sip, then pushed it away. "I'm going to get a Pepsi. Anyone want anything?"

Dan and Karen shook their heads.

She went to the bar. "Where y'all from?" a marine asked her as she waited for the bartender to bring her Pepsi.

"All over the place," Laura replied. He was about her age but looked younger, with his hair cut so short his face looked exposed — not raw, exactly, but uncooked, like bread dough. "We're college students studying in Leningrad. Where are you from?"

"Huntsville, Alabama," the marine said. "So you're learning to speak Russian?"

"Uh-huh. And you?"

"Can't speak a word. Well, okay, I know *hello*, *good-bye*, *please*, and *thank you*. Four words. No point in learning much more than that — I never get to talk to Russians." The bartender gave her a bottle of Pepsi and a glass of ice made from mineral water — safe, non-contaminated ice — and waved away her dollar. "Welcome to Moscow."

When she returned to the table, the hamburgers had arrived. They looked delicious and smelled even better. Dan already had his mouth full and was nodding appreciatively.

"Do you think they have an inner life?" Laura watched the marines carousing at the bar.

"Does who have an inner life?" Karen asked.

She nodded toward the soldiers. "Them."

"Everyone has an inner life," Karen said.

"How do you know? I mean, they come to a foreign country and spend all their time doing pretty much whatever they'd do at home. They don't learn the language or see much of the country beyond what they're forced to see for their jobs. And look at their faces. They look so . . . *unmarked*."

"They're young," Dan said.

"No younger than we are," Laura insisted.

"Do you mean, do they have a soul?" Karen asked.

"I'm not sure," Laura said.

"I think there are people who can spend their lives watching TV and going to work and eating at Burger King and never have a soul-stirring moment or thought, ever," Karen said.

"Their soul might not be stirred, but that doesn't mean they don't have one," Dan said.

The lights dimmed and the movie started. The theme song, "Take This Job and Shove It," blasted through the bar. The marines whooped and cheered. Laura felt uncomfortable. She hadn't said it out loud, but when she talked about an inner life she was worrying about herself: the gaping void she felt inside herself that she wanted to fill with something real, something good. Something she hadn't found at home. The larger life she had come here looking for.

Drama. Passion. Soul.

She'd heard Russians say that Americans had riches but Russians had soul, and she always said it wasn't true.

But what if it was?

Alyosha had soul. That much she knew.

They sat through the movie. She could hardly pay attention to it. Her mind wandered off to memories of Alyosha, memories already, although she'd hardly been away from him for a day.

The way he listened hard as she read a page of Dickens to him, straining to understand the unfamiliar words, enjoying the sound of them anyway.

Lying next to him while the sky outside the window darkened.

Falling asleep while he told her a folktale.

She missed him.

One whole week, she thought. *I'll never make it.*

16

★

A VISITOR IN THE CEMETERY

They spent a lot of time on the tour bus. Irina talked as the bus rumbled through the city from one sight to another, from the Stalinist wedding-cake-on-steroids that was Moscow University to the site of the 1980 Olympics. They passed the classical white columns of the Bolshoi Theater, where they'd be seeing the Stravinsky ballet *The Firebird* later in the week. Irina took them inside the Art Deco department store GUM, or Government Universal Store, a glass-and-metal shopping arcade, to spend money on souvenirs they didn't really want. They rolled along the redbrick walls of the Kremlin and stopped at the Exhibition of the Achievements of the National Economy to admire the gargantuan statue of the Worker and the Collective Farm Woman. He held a hammer, she a sickle, and together they strode into the glorious Soviet future. That night the Americans went to the circus, where they saw a bear riding a motorcycle. They were kept busy every moment, no chance to get up to mischief, whatever that might be.

Laura barely heard a word Irina said. The whole time she stared out the bus window, thinking about Alyosha. Wondering what he was doing. Wondering what Olga was doing. She knew he had been to Moscow several times on trips with his parents and his school, and she wondered how the broad avenues and massive government buildings had looked to him as a boy.

On the third morning of the trip, as the American group lined up to board a bus to the Novodevichy Convent, a flash of blue — a familiar shade — caught Laura's eye. Someone loitered near the hotel entrance, behind a tree, and she glimpsed part of an arm — an elbow — and a bit of fur trim on a parka that looked just like Alyosha's. One sneakered foot stuck out — Alyosha's sneaker?

She stepped out of the line, thinking to dash across the sidewalk and look behind the tree — of course this mystery person couldn't be Alyosha, but she had to make sure. Irina herded her back in line, snapping, "Get on the bus, come on, come on, we're late!"

Laura took a seat next to Karen, leaning across Karen's lap to catch a glimpse through the window of the mysterious stranger.

"What are you doing?" Karen was grumpy from lack of sleep. Actually, everyone was. They'd gone to the hotel bar after the symphony and ended up singing ABBA songs with a gang of

Swedish chemists who were in town for a conference. They closed the hotel bar at two A.M.

"Nothing." The mysterious person had disappeared. Laura felt foolish. Of course it wasn't Alyosha. What would he be doing in Moscow? She was thinking about him too much. It made her see things that weren't there. It made her crazy.

Crazy crazy crazy crazy.

She leaned back for the ride to the convent, while Irina filled them in on the history of the place they were about to see: a sixteenth-century fortress filled with churches, icons, art treasures, and a famous cemetery.

Dan popped up from the seat behind hers. "Did you know Peter the Great stashed his first wife in the convent when he didn't want her anymore?"

"Nice," Laura said.

"That's what convents were for," Karen said. "A place to get rid of unwanted women without having to go to the trouble of killing them."

"Students who are talking in the back," Irina barked over her microphone, "you may want to listen. You are missing important information."

"'Kay, sorry," Dan whisper-grumbled, and Laura and Karen snickered. Irina glared at them.

"Where do they find these guides?" Karen whispered. "They're so cranky."

"They send them to Crankiness School," Laura joked. "The People's Institute of Sullenness Training."

"The Soviet Union," Dan muttered in a mock announcer voice. "Come for the food. Stay for the crankiness."

The three of them broke up in giggles, drawing a glare from Irina that went well beyond cranky.

Laura sleepwalked through the churches, ditching the tour (another glare from Irina) to wander through the cemetery. It was a brisk, breezy, early-spring day, the rawness in the air softening at last. She wove her way through ancient headstones and monuments, pausing at the graves of Chekhov and Shostakovich, Gogol and Bulgakov. She lingered before the tomb of Vladimir Mayakovsky, the poet and playwright who had written "A Cloud in Trousers." The poet Alyosha loved — one of them. The book Alyosha had been reading the first time she met him for coffee.

The headstone was a huge slab of red marble set on a larger slab of gray marble, and in front of it was a bust of the poet, handsome and rakish, his thick dark hair curling over his forehead. She read the dates: 1893–1930. He had killed himself over lost love at age thirty-six.

There it was, that mix of love and death, violence and poetry. Now that she'd found it, she wasn't sure she wanted it anymore. Her heart pounded. In two months, her semester abroad would end. She would have to leave Leningrad, possibly forever. That meant leaving Alyosha, too — possibly forever. Probably forever.

She wanted love without the death, poetry without the violence.

And then, from behind the large marble slab, out stepped Alyosha.

She gasped, terrified at first that she'd really gone crazy. Or that he was a ghost. But he had surprisingly rosy cheeks for an apparition.

"Shhh!" He slipped his cold hands inside her gloves.

"What are you doing here?" She pressed her cheek against his. "Are you real?"

"What? I'm real. I'm real." They stood in the cemetery, cheek to cheek for a long moment, until Alyosha broke apart to kiss her.

"I had to come see you. I couldn't stand to be away for another day."

"But how did you get here?"

"They have a metro in Moscow, too, you know." Eye roll.

"I know. I mean, how did you get to Moscow?"

"I took the train, just like you. Last night. I'm staying with a friend of mine from art school, Dima. Sleeping on his couch."

"And how did you find me?"

He grinned. "You told me you were staying at the Rossiya, so I went there and waited. Before long, out comes a troop of American students who look around my Laura's age, and a tour guide babbling about Novodevichy Convent. And there comes a girl in a sheepskin coat who looks a *lot* like my Laura. And what do you know . . ."

"It is." She kissed him again. "But now what?"

"Now we spend the rest of the week in Moscow together."

"But I can't. I have to stay with the group." They had rules for the trip, just like they had in Leningrad. Everyone must stay with the group, except for designated free periods. Everyone must attend every outing unless they are sick, and then they must get permission from Dr. Stein or Dr. Durant. . . .

"Do you have to stay with them every minute of the day?"

"Well, not when we're free, I guess."

"So? What's on the schedule tonight?"

"The opera. *Eugene Onegin.*"

"And what would happen if you slipped out during intermission and didn't come back?"

"I'd get into huge trouble."

He frowned. "Okay. What's on the schedule for tomorrow?"

She pulled the crumpled mimeographed sheets from her pocket, the itinerary for their week in Moscow. Alyosha noted every hole in the schedule — what few there were — and claimed them for himself. He gave her Dima's address and phone number, with the familiar instructions to be careful when she called. They made a plan to meet the next afternoon in Red Square.

"At St. Basil's." He pulled his hand out of her glove, took her chin in his fingers, tilted it toward him. "One o'clock. Promise."

"At St. Basil's. Promise."

He kissed her. Then he looked up, glanced around, and disappeared among the graves.

She found herself staring at Mayakovsky's head, wondering if Alyosha had really been there, or if she'd daydreamed him into existence. She heard a footstep behind her, turned, and there stood Karen, frowning.

"What's he doing here?" Karen demanded.

She'd seen him.

Karen went on when Laura didn't answer. "Just happened to be in town, I guess?"

"He missed me."

Karen put her arm around Laura's shoulder and began to lead her back toward the museum.

"Be careful, Laura. This guy is making a full-on assault on you."

"Assault?" Laura couldn't understand how Karen could see it that way. "He's not attacking me. This is love."

"Laura, this isn't love. Love lets you go on a trip without following you. Love can live without you for a week, knowing you'll come back."

"No, it can't." The afternoon shadows grew long and cold. In spite of the chill, a heat rose up inside her and flooded her face. "That's how you know it's true love. When he can't live without you."

Karen shook her head. "That's how you know it's obsession. Or something else."

"What else?"

Karen squeezed her shoulders as they walked, as if needing to cushion a blow. "An ulterior motive."

Laura looked down at a worn gravestone. Karen's arm weighed heavily on her shoulder.

"I'm not saying Alyosha's a bad person," Karen said quietly. "But when someone wants something very badly . . . when someone thinks you hold his entire future in your hands . . ." Laura felt her hesitation, her reluctance to finish the sentence. She wasn't about to let Karen off the hook. *Go ahead, Karen. Finish the thought.*

"They won't let it go easily. They'll do anything, convince themselves of anything. Even love."

There it was. What everyone was thinking.

"It's not true." Laura shrugged off Karen's arm and stalked the rest of the way to the museum. "Come on. The bus is waiting for us."

It wasn't true. Alyosha really loved her — for herself. If she were a Russian girl, he'd love her the same, maybe more. She felt it in her skin, her bones, the blood that pumped through her body, from her heart and around and back again. She felt it.

And no one could talk her out of it. Karen meant well, but she didn't know. She didn't know Alyosha the way Laura did.

No one did. And no one knew Laura the way Alyosha knew her, either.

17

★

INTERROGATION

Ivan the Terrible is your favorite czar?" Alyosha was incredulous. "What exactly do you like about him? The murder? The brutality? Oh, I know. It's the insanity, right?"

"Yeah, I do like all that stuff, when it's far back in the past. It makes a good story."

"It might make a good story, but millions of people had to live through it. And die because of it."

"What about this place? He created this, didn't he?" They were wandering through St. Basil's Cathedral, staring at the icons framed in red and gold.

"He had it built for him," Alyosha said. "And then he blinded the architect so he could never build anything so beautiful again."

"See what I mean? Now that's what I call a czar."

"Who's your favorite Politburo leader? Stalin?"

"No. If only Stalin had blinded *his* architects, Moscow would be a lot less ugly."

Alyosha made a mock-horrified face, which melted into a sly grin. "Brezhnev, then?"

"Brezhnev! Too boring." Laura closed her eyes and pretended to snore.

He leaned his cheek against her head so he could whisper ominously in her ear. "I should probably tell you at this point that I'm a KGB agent and you are under arrest."

She jerked her head away, pretending to be alarmed. "What's my crime?"

"Acknowledging the ugliness of Stalinist architecture. Come with me for questioning." He took her hand and led her outside to Red Square, which was mobbed with tourists. The line for Lenin's Tomb snaked halfway around the massive square.

"What are you going to do with me?" Laura asked.

Alyosha looked around at the crowds with annoyance. "There are too many witnesses here. I must take you to headquarters."

Giggling, they ran hand in hand to the metro, which they rode to Old Arbat Street, where Alyosha's friend Dima lived in a run-down but charming old building.

"Here we are." Alyosha opened a door and led her up a winding staircase. "KGB Headquarters."

The apartment was a tiny studio, just a bed, a small sofa, a table, and four chairs, a kitchen off the hall, the walls covered with paintings of Moscow street scenes. Laura took off her coat and sat down on the couch.

"Dima's at work," Alyosha said, putting a kettle on to boil. "Now, my dear . . ." He prowled up to her, towering over her chair. "Let's talk about this problem you have with our beloved leader. You find him boring? Let's see if you find this boring, too —"

He leaned down and kissed her. She kissed him back for a long time. The kettle whistled. Alyosha hurried to turn it off, didn't bother to make the tea he'd planned, and settled down on the couch with her.

The shadows lengthened, then were gone. When they finally came up for air, the room was dark. They lay entwined on the couch, legs and hands and hair tangled together.

"When's Dima coming home from work?" Laura asked.

"I don't know. Maybe late. Are you hungry?"

"A little. What time is it?"

"Seven."

Whoops. She was late for dinner with the group at the hotel. And after dinner, they were supposed to see the Bolshoi Ballet. If she hurried she could make it in time to catch the ballet . . . but she didn't feel like hurrying.

So she didn't.

The next time she checked the clock, it was after midnight.

"Hmm," Alyosha said. "I wonder where Dima is?"

"Does the metro shut down at midnight here, too?" Laura asked.

"It does. But you can get a taxi."

They met Dima coming in on their way out of the apartment. He was blond with a big head and a friendly, open face. "Hey, why don't you spend the night?" he offered.

"I can't. I have to get back to my hotel." She was almost as worried about what Karen would say as she was about being caught away from the group.

"Tomorrow night, then! Good night!"

Alyosha put her into a taxi. She sped through the empty Moscow streets, back to the hotel. Karen was waiting for her in their room, reading in bed. Binky was safely asleep.

"How was the ballet?" Laura asked.

Karen tossed her book to the floor. "Are you kidding me? Are you really going to come in at one in the morning and ask me how the ballet was? Like you care? I was worried about you!"

"I'm sorry." Laura sat at the foot of Karen's bed and squeezed her friend's toes. Karen jerked her foot away.

"Don't. I'm not in a friendly mood. You are in big trouble, girl."

"I am?"

"You'll find out at breakfast tomorrow. If Stein and Durant let you eat."

Laura got up and changed into her pajamas. "Because I missed the ballet?"

"And the Tretyakov Gallery. And dinner. And no one knew where you were. I reassured them there was no need to call the police, and I just hoped I was right."

"You were right. Thank you."

"What's wrong with you lately?" Karen asked. "You've been so . . . reckless. You'll drop anything to see Alyosha. Like you don't care about anything else."

I don't care about anything else, she thought. But she was afraid to admit that to Karen. Afraid that would only bring more scolding, more lectures. "I — I just don't understand why I can't be with him all the time, if I want to."

"And you want to."

"Yes, I want to. Karen, if you only knew him better —"

"All I know is this: If they don't send you home tomorrow, you'll be lucky."

"They can't do that." Laura brushed her teeth and turned out the light. They couldn't send her home, not now.

If they sent her home, she'd be separated from Alyosha forever. And that couldn't happen.

She couldn't let it.

Of course, Karen was right. Before breakfast, Professors Stein and Durant knocked on their door to see if Laura had made it home. When they saw that she was fine, they sent Karen and Binky downstairs to the dining room and gave Laura a talking-to.

Stein and Durant were married, middle-aged, and looked alike. Professor Durant, the husband, was tall and gray with silver glasses. Professor Stein, the wife, was short and gray with silver glasses. They were in charge of the American students studying in Leningrad, but Laura had barely seen them since she'd moved into Dormitory Number Six, and had paid them even less attention. That was one reason she hadn't taken the threat of being sent home too seriously — Stein and Durant did not seem aware of what was going on.

They were not going to let her ignore them any longer.

"Laura, we understand what's going on here," Durant said. "This happens every semester. At least one student falls in love with a Russian who wants to marry her — or him — and move to the States."

"I'm not getting ma —"

"This causes so many problems for the study-abroad program," Stein interjected. "The university officials are always threatening to shut the program down, mostly because of these sham marriages."

"But this isn't a —"

"Never mind the program." Durant set a large hand on his wife's shoulder to indicate that it was his turn now. "What worries me is the heartbreak these marriages cause. The American has to work hard to get her Russian spouse, who has remained behind, out of the country. It's endless paperwork, evasions, a real pain in the ass on both the Soviet and American sides. Once you get him to the States — if you manage to pull it off — you'll have to pass a test proving your relationship is real and not visa fraud."

"That happened to one of our students a few years ago." Stein was beginning to remind Laura of one of the humorless detectives on *Dragnet*, an old TV show. "He married a Russian girl, and once he brought her over, an immigration official judged their marriage a fraud. The girl was deported and our student faced five years in jail as a penalty."

"His parents paid a pretty penny to some high-powered lawyers to keep him out of prison," Durant said.

"The process can take years. By the time the Soviets let your husband out of the country — *if* they let him out — you will hardly know him anymore," Stein said.

"And you're one hundred percent responsible for his welfare. If he can't get a job, too bad. You have to provide for him."

"These marriages almost always break up as soon as the Russian gets his citizenship," Stein added with a meaningful nod.

"You might think he loves you, but we've seen this too many times. The lies, the deceit, the heartbreak —"

"Don't do it, Laura. For your own sake."

"What would your parents say if you stepped off the plane and told them you were married?"

"Well, I —"

"How old are you, anyway? Twenty?"

"I'm nineteen, but —"

"Promise us you won't do anything — apply for a marriage license, go to the embassy for permission — without talking to us first," Stein said. "Do you promise?"

"We're here for you," Durant added.

"Look, I do have a friend." Were they finally letting her talk? Amazing. "But he hasn't asked me to marry him. Or anything like that."

"Yet," Stein said.

"He's already led you away from the group," Durant said. "Your behavior on this trip has been reprehensible."

"I'm sorry."

"Just don't do anything rash."

"Okay. I won't."

The chaperones stood awkwardly in her room, looking at each other as if to ask, *Are we done now?* There seemed to be nothing left to say.

"Are you going to send me home?" Laura asked.

"Not this time," Durant said. "Don't force us to. If you follow the rules from now on, you'll be okay."

"I'll do my best."

"We expect to see you at every activity we have planned for the rest of this trip. Every meal. Every stop. And when we get back, we expect you to attend every class."

They escorted her downstairs to breakfast. After breakfast, before their next field trip, she made a quick call to Dima's apartment and told Alyosha she'd see him back in Leningrad in a couple of days. He didn't take it well. But there was nothing she could do.

18

★

TO THE DACHA

*B*ack in Leningrad, she quickly forgot Stein's and Durant's dire warnings about Alyosha. Or rather, she remembered them, but she didn't care. She saw Alyosha all the time, and weeks passed with him filling her free time with something that felt truly free. The school instituted line after line of things to do, but with Alyosha, she lived between the lines. Before she knew it, April was nearing its end.

Olga and Roma invited her and Alyosha to their dacha in Repino for the weekend. She figured she was in trouble already; she might as well go all the way. She agreed to meet Alyosha at the train station Friday afternoon.

Many Leningraders, even those who weren't particularly well-off, seemed to have a dacha. These ranged from stately country manors, for highly placed Party officials — Laura had heard stories about these secret estates from Alyosha's friends — to tiny, run-down shacks on patches of mud. As long as it was in the country, it was a dacha, and it was beloved. There, city people could escape the neighbors, cook outside, gather mushrooms in the woods, and take in the country air. If Laura was going to understand the Russian soul, she had to see one.

"I'll have to skip Literature again," she told Karen as she packed the night before. Nina was studying late at the library.

Karen sat on her bed, grimly watching her. "You'll notice I'm not saying anything."

Laura crossed the room and kissed her on the cheek. "I appreciate it."

"Doesn't mean I'm not thinking things."

"I know. Want to come with me?"

"No. It may sound strange to you, but breaking the rules while living at the whim of a totalitarian government makes me nervous. I've probably seen *Cabaret* too many times. What will I say if Nina asks where you are?"

"I've got it all figured out. I talked to Dan and he's willing to play my pretend boyfriend. When I'm not in my room, I'm in his, making passionate love to him. There's no rule against Americans dating each other, right? Stein and Durant will be thrilled. Meanwhile, he's with Lena and I'm with Alyosha. It's the perfect crime."

"Hardly. What about Nina?"

"She'll just have to take our word for it."

"I hope she won't ask."

"Who knows? Maybe she won't."

★

Laura met Alyosha at the train station, and they took the *elec-trichka* to Repino. Olga and Roma were already at the dacha, getting everything ready for the weekend. "So the stove will be lit and the cottage will be nice and warm by the time we get there." Alyosha draped his arm around Laura and gave her a smacking kiss on the cheek. "You don't want to arrive when the house is closed and frozen."

"So — there's heat?" Laura asked, a little nervously. She knew better than to take any comforts for granted.

"Of course! An old Russian woodstove. It will warm the whole house. We'll sleep upstairs in the attic. The floor's covered with straw to help insulate it."

"Oh, good." *Straw.* "We'll keep each other warm up there."

"Yes we will, little fish."

They arrived just before dark and walked three quarters of a mile from the station along the edge of a forest. Alyosha knew the way. They entered a small community of ramshackle, makeshift summer cottages, a mishmash of styles and colors thrown together from whatever materials their builders could find. It was a little early for dacha season, so most of the houses were dark. The lights of Roma's house glowed up the road, and smoke curled out of the chimney. The moon rose over the forest of birch trees, illuminating a scene out of a fractured fairy tale.

Roma greeted them at the door wearing a striped felt robe,

an odd furry vest, and waterproof gardening boots. He clutched a bottle of vodka. With his tinted aviator glasses and his devilish grin, he looked a little crazy. "Halloo! Welcome! Come in, come in!" He kissed Laura and Alyosha and hurried them inside to warm up by the stove. Olga greeted them in the kitchen, where she was slicing potatoes.

"We're having a simple supper tonight — just cabbage soup and potatoes and a little cold chicken," she said. "But tomorrow, Roma is making *shashlik*!"

"I make it the best." Roma kissed his fingertips like a cartoon Italian. *Shashlik* was Georgian for grilled lamb shish kebab. "Georgian blood runs through my veins, you know."

"Really?" Laura began to unbundle, taking off her bulky coat and boots. Olga went to a closet stuffed with strange, costume-y clothes, and gave her a quilted housecoat to wear. The stove warmed the kitchen but the rest of the house was still chilly. "I didn't know you were Georgian."

"That explains his hot temper," Alyosha said. Under his coat he wore a down ski vest.

"Where did that come from?" she asked. "All the boys wear them in Providence."

"I don't remember." He wouldn't meet her eye. "I found it somewhere. . . ."

"Someone left it at a party once, remember?" Olga said. "And they never claimed it."

"That's right."

Olga gave Laura a bottle of beer without asking if she wanted one and went back to stirring her pot of soup. "Where's the bathroom?" Laura asked.

Olga frowned. "You should have said something before!"

"I'll show you." Alyosha put down his beer and slipped his feet into a pair of rubber boots. "Put your coat back on."

"And wear Olga's boots," Roma said. "It's muddy out there."

Alyosha lit a kerosene lantern and led Laura outside, past a toolshed, to an outhouse. A wooden pocket nailed to the door held bits of newspaper for toilet paper. He gave Laura the lantern and said, "I'll wait for you out here."

When she was finished, they traipsed back to the house in the dark. A cool wind was blowing the clouds away and millions of brilliant stars blinked down at her.

Supper tasted delicious in the warm kitchen, soup and bread and potatoes and chicken washed down with beer and tea. Afterward they took a bottle of cognac into the living room. Olga lit the kerosene lanterns — the house had no electricity or running water — and they settled on the worn antique sofas and chairs to play cards. Roma reached for his guitar and strummed softly.

"Do you have a dacha in America, Laura?" Olga asked.

"No," Laura said. "We don't have dachas, exactly. But some of my friends have summer houses, mostly at the beach."

Olga shook her head and *tsk-tsked.* "So sad. Cramped up in the dirty city with no place to play in the summer."

It wasn't that bad, but Laura didn't feel like going into it. "Yes."

"I love the way you say *da*," Olga said. She mimicked Laura's American accent. "It's like a kitten speaking. *Da. I'm American. Da.*"

Laura's cheeks got hot. Olga was just teasing, but she was embarrassed. She knew she had an accent but she had no idea it sounded so funny.

"Well, how do you say it? Teach me to say it right."

"*Da*," Roma boomed, coming down hard on the *d* like a heavy knock at the door. "*Da.*"

Laura tried it, lowering her voice and not drawing out the *ahh* like a Southern belle the way she usually did. But this only made them laugh harder.

"Don't worry, Laura," Alyosha said. "It's sweet the way you say it. We like it."

"Yes, it's cute." Olga's smile was sweet as coconut cake, which Laura had always found a little sickening. "Americans are so charming. Like children!"

"Spoiled children," Roma added, as if Laura weren't sitting right there. "Who don't know suffering."

Laura glanced at Alyosha, who shifted on the couch without meeting anyone's eye. He took the guitar out of Roma's arms. "Let me play a song." Laura recognized the song about the Cossack who lost his wild head, and began to hum along. Olga snuggled against Roma and sang, too. She had a pretty voice.

Laura couldn't figure Olga out. She and Roma seemed happy together. So what exactly was her relationship with Alyosha?

"Remember that summer on the Black Sea, Lyosha?" Olga sipped her cognac and smiled dreamily. "We sang that song every night."

"Yes, yes." Roma sighed. "You and your friends camped out on the beach, and you turned as brown as a nut."

"When was this?" Laura asked.

"During art school," Olga replied. "When Lyosha and I were in love."

Alyosha strummed the chords to a new song, as if that would change the subject, but Olga wouldn't allow it.

"You were in love?" The words caught in Laura's throat.

"That's going too far," Alyosha said. "We were together a lot. We were too young to be in love."

"What happened?" Laura asked.

"Olga left me," Alyosha said.

"We had a silly fight," Olga said. "I think it was over some boy I was flirting with. Lyosha got so angry — didn't you? — and wouldn't speak to me for days."

Alyosha concentrated on the strings of the guitar.

"So I said phooey on him and there was Roma," Olga said. "He was waiting for me!"

"We had a little fling," Roma said. He didn't seem bothered by his wife's story at all. He'd probably heard it many times before. And he was probably tipsy from cognac.

"I meant to go back to Alyosha eventually, but by then Tanya had come along. . . ."

"And you got pregnant, so we got married," Roma finished.

Pregnant? So where was their child?

"I had a miscarriage," Olga explained. "So it turns out we didn't have to get married after all, did we, Romachka?"

"No. Turns out we didn't."

Alyosha put the guitar down. "I'll add some more wood to the stove. It's getting chilly in here." He went into the kitchen. Olga smiled, still curled up against her husband, who wrapped his arm around her, apparently content.

At midnight, Laura and Alyosha climbed the stairs to the attic and made their bed on a narrow mattress on the straw-covered floor. Alyosha piled on as many blankets as they could bear. Laura pressed herself against him for warmth and closed her eyes.

"Alyosha?" she whispered.

"Yes?"

"Were you in love with Olga? Back in school?"

"No." He kissed her temple. "She wasn't in love with me, either. We were friends, mostly."

"Is she in love with you now, do you think?"

"No. She's just torturing Roma. She loves to tease people."

"But Roma hardly seems bothered by it at all."

"That's why they're such a good couple."

They lay together in the dark, breathing. An owl hooted outside.

"I don't like the way Olga teases people," Alyosha said. "I could never be in love with her." He shifted so his face was even with hers. She felt his breath brush her lips. "But you are different. You're kind and good. You are exactly the kind of person I could love."

"I'm glad."

"Yes, it's very lucky. Because I do love you."

They nestled together, their breath a buffer against the cold, and drifted off to sleep.

19

★

WRITTEN IN WATER

*I*n her sleep, Laura found herself tilting her face like a flower toward a patch of sun. She blinked and opened her eyes. The attic window was coated with melting frost. Birds chattered noisily in the trees outside, and downstairs, Olga clattered pots in the kitchen and sang to herself. Alyosha was gone, his spot on the mattress still warm. She had to pee badly, but the thought of getting up and going outside to the outhouse kept her paralyzed under the heavy blankets until she couldn't stand it another second.

"Good morning, sleepyhead!" Olga called as Laura hurried past the kitchen to the yard. She waved to Alyosha and Roma, who squatted before a rusty grill, starting a fire. On her way back to the house, Alyosha stopped her for a kiss.

"What are you two doing?" she asked.

"*Shashlik* takes all-day preparation," Roma explained. "The lamb is marinating, and I'm starting the fire early so the coals will be hot as the devil in a few hours."

"I'm his helper," Alyosha said.

"Go inside, helper," Roma ordered. "Go have breakfast with your girl. I ate hours ago."

Laura and Alyosha went inside and sat at the kitchen table, where Olga served them tea, toast, and kasha with milk and sugar.

"This tastes so much better than the kasha at the university cafeteria," Laura said.

"Of course it does," Olga said. "I'm insulted you would even mention my kasha in the same sentence as the university cafeteria."

After breakfast, Laura offered to wash the dishes but Olga wouldn't let her. So Laura and Alyosha dressed up in some of the crazy clothes they found in the closet, things that had been left by relatives and friends over the years — the fuzzy striped vest, a fur hat for Alyosha and a sailor hat for Laura, an old over-coat — and off they tramped, hand in hand, down the rutted, muddy road, through frozen fields strewn with cigarette butts and broken bottles, to the lake.

"Why doesn't Olga like me?" Laura asked.

"What do you mean? Olga loves you!"

"No, she doesn't." She sat on a large rock and stared at the birds picking their way over the melting lake ice. "She pretends to, but it's so transparent. She wants me to know it, too."

Alyosha picked up a pebble and threw it at the water. "She's jealous, that's all. She likes to be the prettiest girl at the party, and when you're around, she's not."

That sounded nice, but Laura didn't think it told the whole story, or even part of it.

"I still think she's in love with you."

"Don't be crazy." He sat with her on the rock and put his arm around her. "What's all this thinking about Olga lately?"

"I get a funny feeling from her," Laura said. "She makes me uncomfortable."

"I'm sorry. Just one more night and we'll be back in Leningrad. Then you never have to see her again."

"Unless I stop by your place uninvited."

Zing. "That's not fair. I couldn't help it that she broke into my apartment."

"You didn't exactly kick her out, did you?"

"Laura, what's behind all this?"

"I don't know." To her surprise, she started to cry. He pulled her close and kissed her salty tears.

She couldn't untangle her emotions. She was crying out of happiness, sadness, confusion, fear . . . and he seemed to sense this. He didn't ask her what was wrong again. She couldn't have given him a coherent answer. Instead, he talked in a low, soothing voice, about dreams.

"I cry a lot, too, Laura. Did you know that?"

She sniffed and shook her head. She'd never seen him cry.

"It's true. At night when I'm home alone in my room, I wish you were there with me. And I think about the future, the future that is coming up so fast, when I will never be able to see you or touch you, or have you next to me. That to me is a terrible future. No matter what happens in the world, if there is nuclear war or starvation or disease, nothing, to me, could be a more terrible pain than that."

She turned her wet eyes to him. He looked back at her tenderly.

"So I cry," he went on. "And to make myself feel better, I tell myself a story. Not a story, exactly; it's more like watching a movie, the most wonderful movie ever made. Do you know what it's about?"

She shook her head. But she knew.

"It's about me in another life. I live in America — in San Francisco, where the weather is warm and there are streetcars like the trams in Leningrad, only cleaner and prettier. Every day I set up my easel on a hill and paint what I see. And what I see is the most beautiful city in the world, beauty all around me in every direction: boats floating under a swaying silver bridge, sunlight sparkling on blue water, houses in fantastic colors dotting the green hills, and beautiful people wearing wonderful clothes like I've never seen before."

She pulled her knees up to her chest and rested her head on them, listening, imagining.

"Then the most beautiful girl of all walks up to me. She says, 'It's time to stop painting now. Come home for dinner.' So I pack up my things and I take her hand and together we walk home through the shining city. And I tell that girl, 'Laura, I am so happy with you. I want our life to stay like this forever.'"

She could see it all. She was crying again.

"I wish that story could come true," Alyosha said. "I would do anything to make it happen. Anything."

She sniffed and wiped her eyes. She felt infinitely happy and infinitely sad at the same time.

"Anything, Laura."

"So would I," she said at last.

"Would you?" He squeezed her tighter, shook her a little. "Would you really do anything to be with me?"

She leaned over and wrote her answer with her finger in the water of the melting lake. He read the word, caught it in the split second before it disappeared: Yes. A promise written in water.

He broke into a wide, ecstatic grin and touched the cold water with one finger, tracing a heart. A cloud passed over the sun, turning the lake gray. "It's getting cold. We should go back." Alyosha stood and helped her to her feet. They walked back to the dacha arm in arm. Something had changed between them. Laura couldn't say what exactly, but she felt it as surely as the quickening wind, the squish of spring mud under her boots, his warm arm in hers.

They ate the *shashlík* at sunset, huddling around the fire in their funny outfits, spearing the lamb meat with shish-kebab skewers and gnawing at it like Cossacks. Laura wiped the grease from her chin, feeling deliciously primitive.

"Laura's already a member of the Lenin Clean Plate Club," Alyosha told Olga and Roma. "But for tonight's valiant achievement in eating, she gets a special commendation."

"Here, here!" Roma saluted Laura with a skewer.

Laura bowed. "The Lenin Clean Plate Award has always been a dream of mine. I want to thank all the little people who helped me get where I am today: my mother, who spoon-fed me mashed peas and stewed apricots; Roma, who cooked this spectacular *shashlik* which inspired me to eat like I've never eaten before . . ."

Olga, Roma, and Alyosha looked slightly baffled by Laura's parody of an Oscar speech, having never seen or even heard of the Oscars, but they knew it was supposed to be funny and laughed anyway.

The sun went down and the cold, sharp stars pierced the blue-black sky. The fire was dying and the cold grew bitter, so they cleared away the food and went inside to warm up by the stove.

"Let's have a seance," Olga suggested. "I can feel the spirits circling the house, waiting to be invited in."

"Olga, no," Alyosha said.

"Why not?" Roma got a large piece of paper and began to draw the letters of the Russian alphabet on it in crayon in a circle. "We'll play the saucer game. That's what we always do in the country." He drew a pyramid and a closed eye in the center.

Laura immediately had a flashback to third-grade slumber parties — the Ouija board. "It's only a game."

"It is not just a game when I play it." Olga took a saucer off a kitchen shelf and set it upside down in the middle of the paper to serve as a planchette. "The spirits come when I call. They don't dare disobey me."

Roma laughed and rolled his eyes. "Queen of the Black Arts, here."

"Queen of the Black Arts" fit Olga pretty well, Laura thought. "How do we play?"

"You go to the door and call to a spirit," Olga explained. "Then we all touch the saucer lightly with our fingertips and wait for the spirit to come answer your question."

"The saucer points to letters on the board to spell out the answer," Laura said.

"You've done this before! I didn't know you were interested in the occult," Olga said.

"Well . . . it was more of a party game —"

"Yes! Exactly. The saucer game," Roma said.

"No, you have the soul of a sorceress, Laura. I see it in your eyes." Olga lit two candles and blew out the lamp. "Who wants to go first? No one? Then I will."

She walked to the front door and opened it, calling, "Cornelius Agrippa! Cornelius Agrippa! Cornelius Agrippa!" She shut the door quickly and hurried back to the table, rubbing her shivering arms.

"Who's Cornelius Agrippa?" Laura asked.

"You never heard of him?" Roma said.

"He was a German magician in the Renaissance," Alyosha whispered. "He wrote books on the occult."

"Ssshhh!" Olga hissed.

"Poor American education," Roma muttered. Laura couldn't tell if he was joking or not.

"Roma, hush! We have to wait for the spirits in silence. Put your fingertips on the saucer."

Everyone lightly touched the saucer. After a moment of silence, Olga intoned, "O Cornelius Agrippa, come to us. Come to me and answer my question: When will I be rich?"

"You always ask the same question," Roma said.

Laura felt a bump under the table that she assumed was Olga kicking Roma in the shin. "Oof!" Roma grunted in confirmation.

The saucer began to vibrate, then move across the wheel of letters. It zoomed around in a circle, stopping at S. Then K, O . . . In Russian, it spelled out *skoro*: soon.

"Soon!" Olga crowed. "Soon I'll be rich!"

"Agrippa always says 'soon,'" Roma grumbled. "He's been saying 'soon' for years."

"Soon," Olga repeated. "Now you try it, Laura. Whose spirit will you call?"

"I'll call Anna Akhmatova," Laura said.

"Good choice," Alyosha said.

"She's very popular," Olga agreed.

Laura went to the door and said "Anna Akhmatova" three times. Then she returned to the table.

"What is your wish?" Olga prompted.

"Can I keep my wish secret?" Laura asked.

"Yes," Alyosha said. "You can ask it in silence."

"But I want to know what it is," Olga said.

"Let her alone," Roma said. "Go on, Laura."

Laura closed her eyes and silently asked, *Anna Akhmatova, will Alyosha and I be together again someday?*

She waited. After a second or two she felt the saucer moving. It landed on a letter. At first she couldn't tell where this was going. But soon the message was clear: *Get married.*

"Really, Anna Akhmatova?" she whispered in the candlelight.

"That's a very interesting answer," Olga remarked.

"It has nothing to do with my question," Laura lied. Why, she wasn't sure. She suspected that Olga controlled the saucer — Olga was the most likely suspect — and wanted to throw her off a little.

"How do you know?" Alyosha asked. "Maybe you can't see the connection yet."

"That's true." Olga's eyes glittered in the candlelight. "Sometimes the spirits' answers don't seem to make sense, but they become clear in the future."

"One day you'll snap your fingers and say, 'So *that's* what Anna meant!'" Roma said. "Now, my turn." He went to the door and called Cornelius Agrippa back. "He's one of the most powerful spirits," he explained as he returned to the table. Then he asked, "Cornelius Agrippa, what will become of our friend Alyosha?"

They sat around the table, perfectly still, as the seconds ticked by. This question seemed to take longer to answer than the others. "Maybe Agrippa's out answering someone else's question at the moment," Laura joked.

"Sshhh!" Olga hissed.

At last the saucer inched across the paper. "A —" everyone said out loud. "-m . . . -e . . . -r . . ."

America.

"America! Isn't that wonderful?" Olga kissed Laura and gave Alyosha a squeeze. "Alyosha's going to America!"

"That's great!" Laura said.

Alyosha smiled shyly and looked pleased, but he wouldn't quite meet Laura's questioning look. Their eyes linked for a split second, magnets catching and pulling apart quickly.

"What are you going to do in America, Alyosha?" Roma asked.

"I don't know."

"Maybe we should ask the spirits," Laura said.

"He'll be an artist, of course," Olga said. "Just like here. Only famous. And rich."

"Rich, rich," Roma said. "For Olga, nothing counts unless you're rich."

They asked the spirits a few more questions — would Olga have a child someday (yes, a girl), would Roma ever own a car (no, a motorcycle), would Laura have children (Olga asked this question for her; the answer was yes, three) — until the game got old and the players sleepy. Laura helped Olga clean up before joining Alyosha upstairs in the attic.

"I warmed up the bed for you," he said as she slipped in beside him.

"Thank you." They huddled together in the dark. "Alyosha — what do you think about that saucer game?"

He squeezed her tighter. "What do you mean?"

"I mean, do you believe that the spirits are really answering our questions?"

"Maybe they are. I know I'm not pushing the saucer around. Are you?"

"No."

Silence.

"But Olga or Roma could be," she said, really meaning *Olga*.

"She wouldn't do that."

"Why not?"

"It's dangerous. That's playing with fate. You don't play with fate."

This struck Laura as a strange and kind of weak explanation.

"So what do you think of the answers they gave us?" she pressed on. "Do you believe they'll come true?"

He hesitated before saying, "I do."

"So you're really coming to America?"

"Somehow I will. I want to."

"And I'm really getting married?"

"Don't you want to?"

"Someday, maybe . . ." He wasn't answering the real question in her mind: Did he connect these two events?

When he finally did fall asleep, she felt sad. He was right there next to her, but she missed him.

What will I do? she thought. *What will I do without him?*

Her life back home flickered in her sleepy mind like a half-remembered dream. Providence. Josh. Classes. All the friends she hadn't bothered to write. All the places she hadn't really missed. How could she go back to that? She was no longer the same person. Russia had changed her, and that empty life would never satisfy her now. That's when she knew for sure — she'd do anything to be with him. Anything he asked.

The next morning, Laura woke up in the attic with straw in her hair. The sun was not up yet, and when it rose it was muffled by clouds that began to pour a spiky, freezing rain on the little dacha. Laura ate a quick breakfast and drank some hot tea and helped Roma and Olga pack up the house, hurrying to catch the next train back to Leningrad.

The four of them trudged through the mud and the sleet to the station, shivering on the platform with a gnarled old man who smelled like sausage and carried his things in a burlap sack. Laura gazed at the forest through a sheet of gray rain.

"They say if it's raining when you leave town, that means someone is sad to see you go," Roma said. "Do you know that superstition, Laura?"

She poked her head out from the warmth of her scarf. "No."

"Who in this village could possibly miss us?" Olga snapped. "No one we know is here."

"Maybe he will." Alyosha nodded at the old man, who picked up a half-smoked *papyrosa* off the ground, examined it, pinched the end, lit it, and started puffing.

When the train came, the old man tossed his cigarette on the tracks and boarded with Laura and her friends. Laura leaned against Alyosha's shoulder and closed her eyes. She knew the Russian landscape was passing by out the window, and it might be the last time she ever saw it. But she was too tired to care. She and Alyosha were together. It was almost May. They had five weeks left. The end of the semester loomed like a black train tunnel, like an abyss.

Every moment they shared together was sweet. And yet every moment brought them closer to the end.

20

★

THE LIGHT'S SOURCE IS A SECRET

I have no idea what Nina thinks you're up to," Karen said when Laura returned from her dacha weekend. "I feed her lies, she pretends — I think — to believe them, and we go back to ignoring each other as usual. By the way, I told her you and Dan are 'pre-engaged.' She thinks that's an American custom where a couple locks themselves in a room for days, refusing to come out."

"That's okay with me." Laura flopped down on her flimsy bed. "Thanks, Karen."

She hadn't been kicked out yet. Maybe Nina wasn't as uptight as she seemed.

May arrived, and with it, real spring. She still needed a coat, but a lighter coat. She didn't need the hat or gloves or boots. The three-foot-deep pack of snow was gone, the daylight stayed and stayed and stayed longer each day, the people on the street were in a better mood, and the whole city felt ready to bloom.

The university was closed for May Day, and Dan organized a group to go watch the parade. She'd seen pictures of the May Day Parade: a grand military spectacle, hundreds of thousands of people marching in the streets, tanks rolling down the avenues, the city decorated in red to celebrate the Triumph of Communism over the World. But she couldn't go with Dan; she had plans to meet Alyosha, who would have preferred to ignore the holiday completely if he could, especially the parade.

"May Day makes me sick," he'd told her. "It's nothing but a huge celebration of Party hypocrisy, a show of military and industrial strength. If we are such a rich and powerful country, why do we all feel so helpless and poor?"

"Let's form our own political party," Laura had suggested, to poke him out of his sour mood. She was thinking of an old Greta Garbo movie she'd once seen, *Ninotchka*, about an uptight Soviet functionary who goes to Paris, where she falls in love and learns to enjoy life. "We'll call it the Lovers' Party and we'll have our own salute. We won't raise our arms or clench our fists. This will be our salute." She kissed him. "I salute you." This struck her as funny, especially since the Russian word for "I kiss" — *tseluyu* — sounded a lot like the English "salute you."

"I like it." He saluted her back. They'd spent the rest of that afternoon vigorously saluting each other.

Looking forward to saluting the Lovers' Party some more, she took the tram from the dorm to Nevsky Prospekt, past buildings decorated with red bunting and Godzilla-sized posters of

Lenin and the current premier, Leonid Brezhnev, as well as images of workers with hammers raised high and farmers brandishing enormous sheaths of wheat. Banners touted catchy slogans like *We Will Carry Out the Decisions of the Twenty-sixth Congress of the Communist Party of the Soviet Union!* and *Let Us Raise Efficiency and Quality!* and *600,000 Bushels of Wheat in the Last Five-Year Plan!* Everyone wore red ribbons pinned over their hearts. Leningrad had begun to feel almost like home, but May Day reminded her that this was another world, enemy territory, not home at all.

Alyosha waited for her at the Summer Garden gate. "Surprise!" He called out as he waved her into the garden, which spring had transformed from a barren, melancholy maze of bare trees into an oasis of budding life. The trees were supple and greening, and marble people lived among them — the statues had finally been unboxed.

"They're alive!" Laura said. "The coffins are gone."

They strolled slowly, so Laura could look at each statue for the first time. There were characters from Russian fairy tales and fables, from Roman mythology, busts of kings and queens and philosophers, allegories like Peace and Victory, Night, Sunset, Midday, Glory, Seafaring, Architecture, Fate; row after row of marble ghosts, cold to touch, heavy, alive in the spring sunlight glinting off the river after their long winter's sleep.

Alyosha took her hand. No gloves to slip into anymore. This was Anna Akhmatova's place, the Summer Garden. Laura recited the end of the poem, her favorite part:

. . . everything is mother-of-pearl and jasper,
But the light's source is a secret.

"The light is really beautiful in June," Alyosha said. "During the White Nights, you can smell the limes and see the sailboats on the river and the swans on the pond. And it never gets dark, not really."

Her student visa expired in early June. By White Nights she would be gone.

Alyosha sat on a bench in front of an odd statue of a naked woman with a bird perched on one arm. The woman had a bawdy expression on her face and the bird was pecking at her breast. Carved in the pedestal was the Latin word *Lusuria*: Lust.

"This was my favorite statue when I was in school," he confessed. "Because of the bird, you know, the way he is pecking at her . . ." He grinned with embarrassment. "It used to make me —" He said a phrase in Russian that Laura didn't understand.

"It what?" she asked.

He blushed. "You know. . . ." He glanced down at the crotch of his pants.

She laughed. "You perv," she teased in English.

"What is *perv?*"

"Guess."

He guessed. She could imagine the effect of the weird image on a teenage boy. And then she felt warm thinking of Alyosha as a boy, just a few years earlier.

"I wish I'd known you then," she said.

"Me too. But you know me now, and that's better than never."

"Much better."

"What were you like at thirteen?"

Laura shuddered at the memory. "I did gymnastics. I was obsessed with gymnastics."

"Gymnastics? Like Olga Korbut?"

Laura nodded. "It's dumb, I know."

"It's not dumb, but I can't picture you . . . you're not like those sad little robot girls, with their exhausted eyes."

"I know. That's why I never got very good at it. I didn't care enough to exhaust myself."

"Better to be a normal person." He kissed the palm of her hand. They watched a young mother push a baby in a stroller down the gravel path, a toddler clinging to the hem of her coat. "When do you leave?"

"June third."

"One month."

"Yes."

"Very soon."

"Too soon."

"It will be unbearable."

The mother and her children rounded the corner and disappeared from sight. A ragged old man sat down two benches away from them, smoking a cigarette and picking at a hole in the knee of his pants.

She was desperate to make Alyosha feel better, to make herself feel better. "I'll write to you every week. And call, too, when I can."

"To call is so expensive. And it's not the same." He pressed her hand between his, the warmth, the smooth skin proof of what a phone call would be missing. "Once you are gone, that's it. You are gone."

"I'll come back someday." She knew that there was no chance he could ever go west to visit her. No chance. Or very, very little chance. Ordinary Soviet citizens were not allowed to travel outside the country; that was just how it was. But she also knew she wouldn't be able to return to Leningrad for at least a year, if ever. He pressed her fingers again, and she felt like crying.

"I have an idea," he said, squeezing her hand harder. "A way we can be together forever."

The tears stalled in her eyes.

He quickly rose to his feet, then dropped to one knee, still clutching her hand. "Laura, will you marry me?"

There it was: the moment she'd been waiting for, and dreading, for weeks.

"I have it all planned out." Not far away, in Palace Square, the May Day celebration was beginning. An old man's voice roared over a loudspeaker, followed by a hoarse cheer. The tone of Alyosha's voice, of the day, had changed. The sense of peace was gone.

"Before you leave we will go to the Palace of Weddings and

get married. Then, when you're in the US, you file the papers to bring me over to live with you. It will take time, but if everything goes smoothly, I can join you in a year. And you will be finished with university by then. We can move to San Francisco, and I'll become a rich and famous painter so you won't have to work. You won't have to do anything. You can spend all day doing just as you like, eating chocolates in our beautiful apartment. . . ."

Laura listened through a fog of shock. She should have expected this, yet somehow she'd been caught off guard.

"We will be rich and free and happy," Alyosha said. "So happy."

Little golden fish, grant me a wish. . . .

He finally stopped talking and gazed up at her, waiting for her reply. His knee was wet from the snowmelt on the ground.

"What do you say? Say yes! Say *da* in your sweet American accent. *Da* . . ."

Her tongue flapped uselessly in her mouth for a few seconds before she managed to work it into a shape that would make sounds.

"But — I'm only nineteen. I'm too young to get married." The word *married* caused a reflexive response in her — *No.* But it was only a reflex, she reasoned. Not a thought. Not an answer.

He rose up off his knee and sat beside her. "Nonsense! Olga married Roma when she was eighteen. Russian girls get married as teenagers all the time. I'm twenty-two; that's plenty old enough to get married."

"And I haven't finished college yet. I have to finish college."

"But I told you — you will be finished before I can emigrate, so it won't be a problem."

"Well —" *Married.* She'd never thought of herself that way before, as *married.* As a wife. Someone's wife. Alyosha's wife . . .

The hopeful look on his face began to harden into a mask of desperation, and that nearly broke her heart. *I love him,* she thought. That was all she could think. *I love him, I love him. . . .*

And he loves me.

Alyosha, sweet Alyosha, he deserved to be happy. He made her happy. They would be happy together.

So why not get married?

Really. Why not?

The more she thought about it, the more it made sense. They were in love. Was there a better reason to get married?

She could bring him to the US to live with her. She could open the door for him, give him opportunities he'd never dreamed of. She could change his life.

She felt a surge of power. He had done so much for her. Shown her Russia, the real Russia, the world of romance and danger, the one she'd been looking for. And he had seen her as no one else had seen her. This was her chance to do something for him. Something big.

And she loved him. He was the love of her life.

"Laura . . . ," he whispered, "I am asking a lot. Maybe you need time to think."

"No," she said. "I know the answer. Alyosha, I will marry you."

21

READING THE FUTURE

*T*he engagement had to be kept secret until they were safely married. Professors Stein and Durant would try to talk her out of the marriage for sure. And if university officials found out, they might expel her and send her home before she had a chance to marry Alyosha. Talking to her parents was out of the question, and anyway, she'd already used up her two allotted calls home.

But she had to tell someone. She was getting married!

"You said yes?" Karen shook her head in disbelief. "Are you crazy?"

Laura had asked Karen to go for a walk with her to give her best friend the big news — in case — in the near certainty — that their dorm room was bugged.

"I knew you'd be skeptical, but I hoped you'd be at least a little happy for me. Don't you like Alyosha?"

"I love Alyosha. Alyosha's great. That's beside the point."

"Is it? Because I kind of thought being great was a requirement for the person I married."

"Laura, you're nineteen. You're still in college."

"I know."

"How are you going to support him?"

"What do you mean? He can get a job —"

"Doing what? His English is sketchy at best, and his only skill is painting movie signs. That job doesn't exist in America."

"He'll be able to do his real art. He can sell that."

Karen stared down Laura until she felt uncomfortable. "You're serious? You think he's going to make a living as an artist in the States? Do you know how hard that is? Do you know anything about the art world?"

"No —"

"Does he?"

"No, but —"

"Neither do I, but I know this much: It's practically impossible to break into, especially when you're a rube from Eastern Europe who's barely even seen any art made after nineteen twenty-five."

"He's smart. He could learn to do something else."

"He'll have to. And until then, you'll have to support the both of you. You'll be legally responsible for him while he learns about banks and checking accounts and credit cards and all these practical things he's never heard of. He doesn't know how to drive. He's never seen a traffic jam. He doesn't know what to say in a job interview, how much things cost —"

"I don't know much about those things, either," Laura protested. "Well, I know how to drive. And how do you know so much about it?"

"From living in the States, watching my parents, growing up there. You know more than you think about it, too. That culture is familiar to you, comfortable. To him it will be another planet. He is going to freak out. And you will have to take care of him as if he's a child."

"I don't care. I love him. Besides, he'll learn fast —"

"And what if you get pregnant?" Karen nearly screamed at the thought. "Then you're stuck with him and a baby?"

"I won't get pregnant," Laura assured her. "I'm careful. I'll keep being careful." She moved closer to her friend, trying to make her see. "You don't understand. Think of what his life will be like if I don't marry him. What will his future be?"

Karen was silent and Laura knew they were imagining the same scenario, because only one was possible: year after numbing year of painting signs for movie theaters and nothing else. A dull, colorless life of shortages, drudgery, waiting, pretending, paranoia . . . He deserved more. They all did, everyone who lived in this messed-up country. But she couldn't help everyone. She could only help him.

"He's the love of my life," she said. "How can I abandon him here? I couldn't live with myself. I'd regret it forever."

"Maybe." Karen looked sad. Laura knew she'd gotten through to her. "But if you marry him and it doesn't go well, you might regret that forever, too."

"I won't regret it. How could I? He's Alyosha!"

Karen shook her head. "We can't read the future. If only we could."

She let herself in with her key, the one he had given her. There was no Olga, thank goodness. The only surprise was the sound of water running in the shower, and Alyosha singing "Only Love Will Break Your Heart" in his adorable accent.

"I'm here!" She popped her head into the steamy bathroom. He peeked out from behind the shower curtain.

"*Rebyonok!*" He gave her a soapy kiss. "I'll be out in a minute."

She took off her coat and went into the kitchen. A vase of red roses decorated the table. She couldn't help but notice the very small package on the table beside the vase.

He came out of the shower all warm and damp, his hair spiking out as he rubbed it with a towel. He grabbed her and kissed her. She pressed against him and kissed him back. He was already naked, his skin damp and warm and smooth, so stumbling over to the bed and falling down onto it was the natural thing to do.

She peeled away her clothes — sweater, turtleneck, corduroys, bra, panties, socks — until they were both naked on the cool sheets and under his scratchy blanket. He kissed her over and over, gently and softly. His skin felt springy, almost rubbery, resilient. He had a dimple on each hip, where the muscle cupped inward, and she rested her hand there. She wished she had a muscular dimple like that, wished her hipbones jutted like his, but he seemed to like her pillowy softness, so it was okay.

After a while, they lay side by side in bed, watching the darkness deepen outside the window. He held her hand. She thought, *Soon this man will be my husband.* The word *husband* sounded strange, too adult. But she'd get used to it. And after a terrible year or so when they must be apart, he'd come to her and they'd be together forever.

She couldn't imagine a day when she wouldn't feel happy about that.

"Stay here." He got up and padded barefoot into the kitchen. The light went on; she saw a yellow square of it against the bedroom door. In a few minutes, after some shuffling, he returned with a glass of water and the small box.

"I bought this for you. I hope you like it."

She unwrapped the box and opened it. Inside was a plain silver ring. Engraved along the inner rim were the Russian words *To Laura with love from Alexei.*

"For our wedding," Alyosha said.

She slipped it over her ring finger. "It fits."

"Good." They kissed again to seal their pact. *We are married now, whatever happens*, she thought. She didn't know why those words came into her mind — *whatever happens* — but they did.

He put the ring back in the box, to save for their wedding. They dressed and started fixing dinner. While he cooked, Alyosha explained what would happen. As soon as possible — tomorrow, if she could — they would go to the Palace of Weddings to register and set a date for the ceremony. This had to be done at least two weeks before the wedding, so there was no time to waste. Then, in about two weeks, they'd return to the palace for the ceremony. She could bring Karen as her witness, and he would invite Olga and Roma. "Afterwards we'll go to a restaurant and have a little party, with champagne." He'd ask his father to come, too, but Alyosha doubted he'd respond.

Laura thought of her own parents with a stab of regret. They wouldn't see her get married. They'd be sad about that. Once Alyosha arrived, surely they'd throw a big party for the new couple. It wouldn't be the same as a real wedding ceremony, but there was nothing to be done.

"If my father met you, maybe he'd change his mind about me," Alyosha said. "He would take one look at you and fall in love, like I did. How could anyone not fall in love with you?"

"Believe me, it's possible." But she laughed, not caring who loved her, as long as Alyosha did.

22

★

DRESS SHOPPING WITH OLGA

"I knew it from the beginning." Olga met Laura outside the Passage department store to help her shop for a wedding dress. "From the first time I met you, I knew you were the one for him." She grabbed Laura and kissed her cheeks three times. "I'm so excited! Perhaps someday Roma and I will come visit you in San Francisco!"

"I hope so." They went inside and Laura eyed the dresses in the shop windows skeptically. They were so shiny and cheap-looking. She didn't want to wear a traditional wedding dress, just something nice, and the two baggy dresses she'd brought with her weren't appropriate for a wedding.

A wedding. The nerves were beginning to get to her.

"I think you should wear blue," Olga said. "With a matching corsage."

A corsage. It sounded like prom wear. They walked into Dress Shop Number Three — how it differed from Shops Two and One wasn't clear — and looked at a blue polyester dress on a mannequin. "Here it is." Olga pulled another dress off a rack. "Go try it on."

A salesgirl led Laura into a dressing room. She sat down on the bench and sighed at herself in the mirror. This wasn't how she'd imagined her wedding preparations, when she'd bothered to imagine them. Her marriage would be witnessed by three people she'd known only a few months. They were lovely people, but they weren't part of her history, her real life. Her parents wouldn't be there to see her get married. Or her brother, or her roommate, or any of her friends from high school or college. They wouldn't even know about it until she got home. Surprise! She wondered how they'd take it. It wouldn't matter anyway, because the deed would be done.

None of that matters, she told herself. *What matters is that I'll get to be with Alyosha again. Someday.*

She tried on the dress and twirled in front of the mirror. She'd never wear this normally. She stepped out of the dressing room to show Olga.

"Gorgeous!" Olga and the salesgirl clapped when they saw her. Olga had taken off her vinyl coat and draped it over a chair. She was wearing a tight pair of Calvin Klein jeans — the first pair Laura had seen in Leningrad.

"Where did you get them?" Laura asked as Olga modeled them proudly.

"From Alyosha, of course." Olga kept her voice low, one eye on the salesgirl. "For my last birthday."

"From Alyosha? But how did he get them?"

"How do you think he gets any of his stuff?" Olga stopped to look at a frilly orange chiffon dress that Laura wouldn't be caught dead in. "The records, the books, the clothes? From his American friends."

"What American friends?" Laura asked. She'd never seen him with any Americans other than Karen and Dan.

"You know," Olga said. "Like you." Laura blinked at her. "Every semester, when a new group of American students arrives, Alyosha makes a new *friend*."

Laura flinched.

"They come and they go," Olga said with studied casualness. "We've been hoping he'd find a girl to marry him and take him away from here, but none of them would do it. Until you! Lucky you!"

"What do you mean?"

"I mean, every semester, when the new students arrive, he waits outside the university gates and . . . you know . . . picks one out."

"But — we met by accident —"

Olga laughed, but her laughter slowed when she saw that Laura wasn't joking. "Sweetie. You don't believe that?"

Laura sat down. "No!" the salesgirl shouted. "You can't sit down in that dress until you buy it."

Laura stood and walked stiff-legged back into the dressing room. Whatever else she did that day, she would not be buying a wedding dress.

She slowly unzipped the blue dress. The zipper snagged. She pulled the dress over her head anyway.

The gypsies. That first day, he had rescued her from the gypsies. It had been so chivalrous, so lucky. Fate.

Or so she had thought.

Olga's words sank in like a punch in the stomach. Alyosha loved her! Didn't he? Had it all been a lie?

Was he just like Lena, the cold-hearted ballerina, after all?

Scenes of the past few months replayed like a movie in her mind. She watched those moments — when she'd been so happy — and was overwhelmed by waves of sadness, enough to drown her.

She'd been foolish. Really, she hardly knew him. She'd met him in January, and here it was, May. She was living in a foreign country where she didn't understand everything people said, why they did what they did, it was all so strange to her, and she didn't know what she was doing. . . .

Why was she getting married to a stranger?

She was at his mercy. She was lost.

She put her own clothes back on and walked out of the store without looking at the salesgirl or speaking to Olga. She just left.

"Laura! Wait!"

She ignored Olga's shrill, birdlike call. She walked through the department store and out onto the street. She hardly saw where she was going. The people who bustled in front of her barely registered. That was why she bumped right into him.

Alyosha.

"Laura! Have you found a dress yet? Don't show me; I want to be surprised. . . ."

She couldn't speak. She looked at his face, the eyes she loved, trying to see evidence of the truth she now knew. Where was it? Where was the hard-heartedness that would allow him to lie to her, use her, deceive her for his own gain? She couldn't see it.

"What's the matter?" He held her by the shoulders, looking into her face. His eyes moved beyond her to someone on the street. Someone who she knew must be Olga, looking horrified or at least embarrassed. "What happened?"

He released her and something snapped.

"I know what you're doing," she said quietly. "I'm one of a long string of American girlfriends, the dumbest one of all, because I fell for your tricks. Or almost did. I know I mean nothing to you. Soon you will mean nothing to me."

She broke away and ran up Nevsky Prospekt. Alyosha shouted and chased her. She saw the Astoria Hotel up ahead. As she'd done so many times to avoid pesky Russian harassers, she flashed her passport and went inside, went to a place where he couldn't follow.

23

★

CHANGE OF HEART

If you look for the answers to your soul's deepest problems, your everyday happiness will be destroyed.

This thought occurred to Laura during a discussion in her Monday afternoon Russian Literature class, so she scribbled it down in her notebook. They were reading *Oblomov*, by Ivan Goncharov, a nineteenth-century novel about a "superfluous man" who did nothing but lie on a couch all day long, eating, sleeping, and fretting about the changes imminent around him. He was paralyzed by his fear of change, and that paralysis eventually killed him.

But if examining your life led only to misery, what was the alternative? Stumbling blindly along, hurting people and being hurt without thinking, without learning how to live better?

"Laura, your problem has nothing to do with the unexamined life," Karen said. "Or the examined life. It has to do with material reality. You have something someone else wants: a US passport. He does what he can to try to get it. You decide whether you want to share it or not."

Karen had not turned out to be the type of friend who resists saying "I told you so" when she is right. Laura couldn't blame her. Now that she saw the Alyosha situation for what it really was, what it had been all along, she felt like an idiot.

Because she had been an idiot.

And she was still an idiot. Because even though she was furious, angry, humiliated, and ashamed . . . she still loved him.

And if she could carry a contradiction like that inside her, maybe he could, too. In spite of all the evidence to the contrary, she couldn't quite believe that he didn't love her. Her head repeated it like a drumbeat — *he doesn't love me, he doesn't love me, he doesn't love me* — but her heart could not accept it.

When classes ended, she and Karen walked across the campus, past the *OGNEOPASNO!* wall, and through the university gates. Laura paused involuntarily — half expecting that Alyosha might be lurking nearby, waiting for her. Karen read her mind and tugged at her elbow.

"Come on, *devushka*. No moping, no hoping. Just keep walking."

They crossed the Builders' Bridge, where the gypsy women gathered, their babies all still babies, not one of them having gained a pound.

At the memory of that first day with Alyosha, her heart lurched and ached. She'd treasured that memory, the meet-cute story she would tell her children, and now it was a sham.

"What did you do to these poor gypsies, anyway?" Karen asked. "They won't even look in your direction."

"The secret password is *militsia*," Laura said.

"Hmm." Karen nodded as a truck loaded with clean-shaven, uniformed young militiamen rumbled by. They lounged in the back of the truck, machine guns resting casually over their shoulders. "Makes sense."

Below the bridge, the gray waters of the Neva River flowed smoothly at last to the sea, free of ice and smelling of brine. The city sparkled in the sunlight, pastel walls and golden spires glinting like jewels. "Too bad we have to leave now that it's finally warm," Karen said. "In January I couldn't wait for May, but now that it's here —"

"I know," Laura said. "We feel like we belong."

"I wouldn't go that far, but yeah, sort of."

When they reached the dorm she paused at the door, staring down the street toward the phone booth, blocks away, that she had used to call Alyosha. The man with black glasses — was that him? He looked different without his fur hat — rounded the corner with his dog, ambling in the direction of the phone booth. He stopped to let the dog pee in the gutter. He was just a dog walker, she decided. No threat to her at all.

Karen put an arm around her and led her gently inside. "You're better off this way, and you know it."

★

Before school, after school, she looked for him every day, but he was never there. Soon all she cared about was seeing him again. She was heartbroken and angry and she wanted to confront him one last time. Let him try to explain his way out of it. She would tear his explanation to shreds and then leave, finally satisfied. On Friday, she took the keys he'd given her and went to find him.

24

★

EMPTY

*A*lyosha was usually home from work by that time, play-ing records and painting before dinner. She paused outside his door, took a breath, listened. The hallway was quiet, the apartment was quiet. She knocked.

Quiet.

No one came to the door. She knocked again.

The elevator clicked, hummed, rattled. She heard the car ris-ing through the building, stopping somewhere, perhaps the floor below. The door clanked open, clanked shut.

Silence.

She took out her key and unlocked the apartment door. It swung open, bumped the coat rack with a muffled *ump*. A pale square of sunlight leaked into the hall from the bedroom window.

"Alyosha?" she called. She stepped inside.

The apartment was empty. The breakfast dishes — a tea

glass, a small plate, a knife and fork — were clean and dry in the dish drain beside the sink. The bed was neatly made as always. Everything looked fine. Surely he would be home soon. She took off her jacket and shoes and sat on the bed to wait for him.

A painting stood propped on an easel in the corner across from the bed. It was a new one; she'd never seen it before. It was a portrait of her.

She sat motionless in the silence, staring at the picture. He'd painted her in her favorite blue sweater against a bright background of heavenly blue. Light glowed behind her head, giving her a halo. She was half smiling, not happy, not sad, but confused and thoughtful.

He loved her. The love was in the picture. He'd painted love all around her, on her face, in her hair, in the shade of blue he chose, in the light that bathed her.

Her anger melted away. She didn't care why he had asked her to marry him. She didn't care whether his love was real or tainted by his desire to leave.

She still loved him.

She felt ashamed. Alyosha was good. She understood why he wanted to leave, and she didn't blame him for doing anything he could to get out. She could still help him, if he let her.

She would wait for him.

My time in Russia is coming to an end, she thought as she sat and stared in a trance. *Soon this will all be gone.* The rough wool blanket on the bed. The low tea table. The guitar in the corner, the old folk songs. The carefully tended shelf of rock-and-roll records, the well-dusted East German stereo. The tiny plaster squares painted with exquisite scenes of Leningrad street life: stray cats; bloated babushkas sweeping rubbish in alleys; mysterious archways and doors; old men in wool caps smoking *papyrosi*; girls looking beautiful in ill-fitting clothes. *I will leave, and this will all disappear in a cloud, like a dream. This room will be a place I once saw in a dream, and perhaps will see again in a dream, but never as real and solid as this. I will go back to my world in another dimension, a parallel world where none of this is real.*

She sat and waited as the evening light faded and grew fuzzy. She lay back on the bed and fell asleep.

She woke up suddenly in total darkness, except for two glowing lights in the room — the clock radio beside the bed and the green light on the stereo. It was nine fifteen.

She sat up. Alyosha had not come home.

She crossed the room to the stereo. A Neil Young record sat on the turntable. It was not like him to leave the stereo on, or even to leave a precious record out of its case.

She pushed the OFF button and the green light went out. She turned on the overhead light. Alyosha had not been there all day.

She had to get back to the dorm. Maybe he'd gone to Olga and Roma's after work, for a party or something, she told herself as she put on her sneakers and coat. She tried not to worry. But something wasn't right.

★

She went back the next afternoon. Everything in the apartment was just as she'd left it. The same dishes in the drain. The same record on the stereo. He hadn't been home.

Where was he? She didn't know what to do. She looked in the refrigerator and took out some eggs. She made eggs for herself, and tea, and spent the evening watching the light fade over the trash-strewn field outside his window. She propped one of her shoes against the door, in case someone sneaked in while she slept — she'd know the door had opened if her shoe moved. When it was completely dark, she got undressed, slid under the covers, and went to sleep.

She woke up early in the morning. No one had come in while she slept. Her shoe was propped against the door right where she'd left it.

Anxiety gnawed at her. Could he have gone to the dacha? But what about his job?

She dressed and hurried to the subway to get to the university in time for her first class. The metro was packed for the morning rush. The metro car smelled like sausage and stale breath and tobacco. Two old men stood near her in dirty work clothes, pickled in vodka. Everyone stared at her, just as they always did. She wanted to glare back, to stick out her tongue, to spit at them, to kick their fat shins. She hated them. She was so tired of being watched, of feeling strange, of smelling their stinky body odors. She was sick of their bad teeth, the fatigue on their faces, their weary slumping and pushing and shoving. Peasants. That's what they were. Peasants who didn't know how to take care of themselves, who needed authoritarian father figures to tell them what to do, who worshipped order and control over everything else, who had no imagination, who wouldn't know what to do with freedom or choice if they had it. Their leaders bossed them around, and in turn they bossed one another around, passing brutality down from stronger to weaker until the weakest could barely stand being conscious and took refuge in a fog of drink. If they had heroin here, Laura thought, this would be a land of junkies.

She ran to the Philology Department and reached her Phonetics class just as the last bell rang. Karen waited for her in the hall, worry on her face.

"What happened last night? Did you find him?"

"No."

"So what were you doing? Nina went to Dan's room and saw that you weren't there. She said she's going to report you this time. She's probably already done it."

"Let her. What can they do to me now? We're leaving in a week anyway."

Semyon Mikhailovich came out and prepared to close the classroom door. "No gossiping, girls. Let's get ready for class."

Karen and Laura went in and sat down with Dan and Binky. *Where do you think he is?* Karen wrote in English in Laura's notebook. Laura just shook her head and wrote *?????*

25

★

RANSACKED

*T*his happens, you know." Dan walked back to the dorm with Karen and Laura after class. "People disappear. Sometimes they come back, shaken and cowed. And sometimes they don't."

"But why him?" Laura had heard plenty of scary stories about people being arrested for no apparent reason. But she still wanted a reason. "He hasn't done anything wrong."

But deep down she knew why he might be in trouble. He'd fraternized with foreigners. With her. And this was the answer she saw in Dan's and Karen's faces, too.

"I can't leave without knowing he's okay."

"Go back and check on him again. Maybe he's home by now," Karen said.

"And what if he's not?"

"Do you know any of his friends?" Dan asked. "Maybe they can tell you something."

Roma and Olga — if anyone knew anything, they would.

★

She went to Alyosha's first — one last time, hoping he'd be there. She let herself into the apartment without bothering to knock. "Alyosha?"

This time, things were different. Someone had been there.

The place had been ransacked. In the kitchen the cupboard doors hung open, broken dishes littering the floor. An egg dripped down the wall, among bits of shattered shell. In the bedroom, the drawers had been emptied, his clothes and paints strewn everywhere. Laura stepped over a pile of socks and underwear. The books and records were gone. The painted tiles were smashed, the canvas paintings ripped. The portrait of her stood slashed and tilted on the easel.

"Alyosha . . ." She sank onto a pile of papers and cried.

She went back to the center of town to find Roma and Olga. She remembered where they lived — she and Alyosha had stopped by their apartment on one of their walks. She rang their buzzer, and Roma let her in. He had just gotten home from work. Olga was starting dinner.

"Laurenka, Laurenka." Olga kissed her on both cheeks. "Come in. You'll stay for dinner."

"I'm not very hungry —"

"Nonsense." Olga set a third place at the table.

"I'm worried about Alyosha —" Laura began, but Olga stopped her, waving a scolding finger in her face and shaking her head.

"Not here," Roma whispered. They assumed their apartment was bugged.

"It's a nice evening," Olga said. "Maybe you and Roma would like to have a walk before dinner."

Roma led her outside. They walked along the Moika Canal, the narrow streets once prowled by a sleepless, tortured Dostoyevsky.

"Have you heard anything from him?" Laura asked. "Do you know what's happened to him?"

"No. I tried to call him, and when he didn't answer after two days, I went to see him. He didn't answer the door. His neighbor, a cranky old woman, peeked out and glared at me with suspicion. I hoped perhaps he'd gone away somewhere with you, some romantic trip."

"I was at his place just now," Laura said. "Someone's been in there. They tore it apart."

Roma plucked at his mustache, nodding as if none of this surprised him. "You must stay away from Avtovo. They are surely watching his building to see who comes and goes, and you are not helping him by going there."

"I didn't realize. . . ."

Roma muttered something she couldn't quite hear.

"What?"

"Don't look for him," Roma advised. "He knows where to find you. Just wait. If he wants to contact you — if he *can* contact you — he will."

"But the semester is almost over. We're leaving next week."

"Give me your address. I will write to you if I hear anything."

"I can't leave like that," she insisted. "I can't leave without seeing him again. I have to know what happened. Maybe we can still get married, if he comes back soon enough —"

Roma shook his head. "Not this time. You'll have to come back."

They walked in silence along the canal. Every curve in the water, every ripple, saddened her.

"Roma," she pressed. "What do you *think* happened to him?"

Roma kept his eyes on the cobblestone street, his worn shoes, and their threadbare laces. "I think his life may be more complicated than you understand. His relationship with you, and wanting to leave, and all his black market American clothes and books and records, and his unacceptable dissident art — none of those things are in his favor. But anything could have happened. One of his neighbors might have seen you at his place too many times and accused him of colluding with foreigners. Someone might be trying to get at his father, or his father might have turned him in for some reason. One of his friends might have betrayed him, as revenge for some perceived slight. He might have been arrested for a crime he is completely innocent of. It doesn't matter, because he doesn't *look* innocent. He is not a member of Komsomol. He avoids all Party activities and in fact makes fun of them. He lives on the fringes of society. His tastes are decadent: rock music, T-shirts, American books, American girls . . . If the authorities want to harass him, they have plenty of reasons to do it. And they don't need a reason."

He turned around and they headed back toward the apartment. "Are you hungry yet? Let's have dinner. Olga's making cutlets."

"This is all my fault. I have to make it right somehow."

"Laura, my dear, that is not in your power. You must do as you're told. You have no choice. American temper tantrums will not do you any good right now. Accept your fate and his, and go home to your plush and easy life. You will forget about us soon enough."

He stopped in front of his building and held the door open for her. She shook her head. "Thank you. Maybe another night. Tell Olga good-bye for me."

She walked down the street and turned toward the river. Roma was wrong. She would never forget about them. She was insulted he would think so.

26

★

LITTLE GOLDEN FISH, GRANT ME A WISH

*T*he American students took their final tests and received Certificates of Achievement at a special ceremony in the great hall at the university. They packed up their stuff, said good-bye to their friends, and prepared to fly home to the States. The semester would be over in five days.

Laura felt disoriented, waking from one dream to find herself in another dream, where nothing felt real. She wrote an essay, she studied her vocabulary and memorized her Pushkin, but whether any of this was sinking in, she had no idea. She lived in a fog of heartbreak and guilt and all she could think was *Alyosha Alyosha Alyosha.*

She stood up from the round table in her dorm room and stretched, walked to the window, and looked out at the street. The tram rumbled past on its way over the Builders' Bridge. The river flowed, calm and blue. Laura remembered her first view out this window, the snow piled along the streets, the sparks from the tram glowing in the frosty air. Now it was spring. Everything was different.

"I need a break," Laura told Karen. "Want to take a walk?"

Karen looked up from *Oblomov*. "No, I never want to leave my couch, ever."

"Seriously, Count Oblomov."

"Seriously. This book makes me feel lazy."

"I'm going out. Want anything?"

"Cookies. You know the ones."

They were addicted to these puffy, soft cookies with a sweet white glaze. She put on her jacket and went outside. The city shined. She caught the tram over the Builders' Bridge, across Vasilievsky Island and over the Palace Bridge. She got off in front of the sleek, space-age Aeroflot office on Nevsky and started walking. She didn't think about where she was going until she recognized the bronze globe of Dom Knigi a block away.

She went inside, one last time. She wandered the aisles, staring at old manuscripts and maps protected by glass cases. She found herself drawn to the poetry section. And there he was.

For a second she thought she was seeing a ghost. He was thin and pale, his hair shaggy and dirty, with deep circles under his eyes. Alyosha gave her a sad smile and put his finger to his lips. He was holding a copy of Anna Akhmatova's poems. He put the book down on the shelf, still open to a page. Then he slipped away.

She wanted to shout, *Wait!* but she didn't dare. She went to the shelf and looked at the book. He'd left it open on "Summer Garden."

She closed the book and put it back on the shelf. Then she left the shop and walked up Nevsky toward the river.

He was waiting for her in the Summer Garden, under the funny statue of Lust, the woman with the bird on her arm. She nodded at the spot next to him on the bench — was it okay to sit there? — and he nodded back. She sat down beside him. He touched her hand briefly, then pulled away.

"It's okay to be seen with me?" she asked.

"No," he said. "But this is okay, for a few minutes. We are simply two strangers occupying a park bench."

"What happened to you? Where have you been?"

He tucked his hands into his pants pockets. "I was arrested by the KGB. They questioned me about you and many other things. Some things I know nothing about. But that is normal."

She'd known this was probably what had happened, but she couldn't hold back a gasp, the nervous pace of her heartbeat at the word *arrested*.

"Alyosha, I'm sorry. It's my fault."

"My sweet Laura, it is not your fault. None of this is your fault. Someone reported me for antipatriotic activities, and I can't deny that I have engaged in quite a few of those. Not all of which are you."

"But who reported you?"

"I don't know. It could be anyone."

Laura thought of Nina. Could Karen have let something slip to Nina, or to one of their professors? To Stein and Durant, who would certainly want to stop her from marrying on their watch?

Or Olga, she thought, and she didn't know why. She could imagine Olga betraying a friend, if she had a reason.

Her own thoughts made her shudder. How had this happened? She was suspicious of everyone.

"It's true. I like Americans," he said. "I like being friends with them. They're funny and crazy and they're not afraid. They talk about interesting things, things we never hear about here, like new music, all the strange things one can eat, what's happening in the rest of the world. They think everything is funny. And they really are my friends, and they weren't all girls, you know. Lots of times I picked out a guy to be friends with, if he looked like someone who loved rock music or art."

She nodded and bit her lip.

"But you are different. I'm in love with you. That never happened with the other Americans. It has never happened to me before, with anyone."

Her breath caught in her throat.

"I understand your dilemma," he went on. "You think I want

something from you. You see it all around you. People will do anything to get what they want. They are petty and ruthless. They will turn in their own cousins to get an apartment, they will knock a woman to the ground for a piece of meat. They lie and cheat, and when something valuable crosses their path they take it quick, before someone else does. I'm Russian, too. Why should I be any different?"

He stopped there. He did not claim to be different. He did not defend himself. His brown eyes were wet and they looked straight into hers, not defiantly but affectionately.

Nothing about him was petty or ruthless or greedy. She couldn't read his mind, but she knew how he had treated her from the first day they met: kindly and generously. Always.

"So — you are free now? Will everything be all right?"

He nodded, but he looked so drawn and tired. He looked ten years older. Her dear Alyosha.

"You're so thin," she said. "Delicate and wispy. Like a cloud in trousers."

"I am a cloud in trousers, transformed by love for you."

The first time they met in the bookstore felt like years ago.

"I still want to marry you, Laura. More than anything. I wish we could get on a plane and fly straight to San Francisco right now."

"I will marry you," she whispered, desperate and hoarse. She wanted to shout it. "I will marry you, Alyosha. I'll do anything to save you."

He pulled his hand from his pocket and swiped it over hers, pressing her palm for a second. "It's too late, little fish. I have a record of dissident activity now. Even if you marry me, the authorities will never let me leave. You will apply and apply for my exit visa, over and over again for years. And year after year they will say, 'No, he cannot leave, he is a criminal, a dissident, he must stay here where we can watch him. . . .'"

The tears came without effort, filling her eyes to their borders and spilling over down her face like a river recently thawed.

"Still, we could try," she said.

He nodded sadly. "We would have had a beautiful life together in California. I would find us an apartment with a view of the bay, and every day I would make a new painting of you, bathed in sunlight."

She'd once resisted the idea of marriage, but now it sounded lovely to her, and she longed for this fantasy life he described more than she'd ever longed for anything.

Alyosha continued. "Someday, through some miracle, I will get there."

"I'll meet you there, Alyosha."

They sat in silence for a few minutes, crying. She wished she could throw her arms around him and cover him with kisses, drink up his tears, but she didn't dare. The park was green now, birds sang melancholy songs in the trees, and couples strolled arm in arm down the lanes. The green, the birds, the spring made the moment even sadder than it would have been in the ice and snow. Everything was open, ready to bloom, but they had to hide, keep their feelings to themselves amidst this beauty.

"I remember the night you told me the story of the fisherman and the little golden fish," she said at last.

He smiled. "You fell asleep before the end."

"That's right — I never heard how the story ends. Will you tell me the end of the story?"

"Well, you remember how it begins, right? The fisherman catches a little golden fish who can talk, and the fish offers to do him a favor if the fisherman will free him. But the kind fisherman frees the fish without asking for anything. When the fisherman's wife hears about this, she sends the fisherman back to find the fish and ask for bigger and bigger things —"

"A new washtub, and then a house, and then to be a lady, and a *czaritsa*," Laura said. "*Little golden fish, grant me a wish.* . . . I think that's where I fell asleep."

"The fisherman's wife finally asks to be ruler of the sea and all its denizens, including the golden fish himself. This is too much. So without a word the golden fish swishes his tail and swims away, deep into the sea. And when the fisherman goes home there is nothing left of his wife's wishes. She sits on the steps of their old shack, holding the broken-down washtub. They had found a golden fish, a fish who could grant wishes, but in the end they are left as poor as they began."

He sighed.

"We're leaving on Saturday," she said. "When will I see you again?"

He didn't speak, just shook his head and pulled a small package out of his coat pocket. It was wrapped in brown paper and tied with string. "Open it when you are alone."

She took the package. It was the length of her finger, square and flat, like a tiny painting. "Is it okay if I write to you?"

"Please write to me. I don't know if I'll get your letters, but try. And I'll write to you, too, every week."

"I promise to write every week, too."

"You'd better go now. You leave first, and I'll go later."

"No —"

"Laura, don't worry about me. I'll be fine. But you must go now. Please go. And hide the gift I gave you well. Find someplace in your suitcase where customs won't look too hard."

"Okay."

"I love you, Laura."

"I love you, too."

She kissed one fingertip and pressed it against his cheek. Then she stood up and walked away. She wanted to turn around and look at him, but was afraid to. When she passed through the garden gates, she turned at last and saw him sitting alone on the bench.

I may never see him again, she thought, and her heart cracked like a mirror.

★

Back in her room, she unwrapped the package. It was a tiny painting of her and him, standing together in an airy apartment, in front of a window. Nearby was a table set for dinner with golden plates and lots of food — a whole fish, green salad, a bottle of wine, a bowl of grapes. He had his arm around her and she fitted against his side, her head on his shoulder. He kissed the top of her head and she glowed like a saint in an icon. Through the window behind them: a broad blue sky with two puffy white clouds, a bay dotted with sailboats, and the Golden Gate Bridge.

27

★

CUSTOMS

*H*er end-of-term report card was mixed, to put it politely. She got a 5 in Phonetics and Conversation, a 3 in Translation, a 4 in Grammar, a 2 in Composition, and a 1 in Literature. Semyon Mikhailovich, her Phonetics professor, wrote: *Laura clearly enjoys learning idioms, songs, and poetry and takes great care with her pronunciation. Somehow she picked up a lot of idiomatic Russian phrases and slang on her own. She was a delightful student.*

Yeah, *somehow.* On the other hand, her Literature professor commented: *Laura Reid missed almost half her Literature classes, particularly when they fell on Friday afternoons. When she was present, she rarely participated in discussion because she hadn't done the reading. Therefore, I failed her.*

This was the first failing grade Laura had ever received, but she accepted it with a shrug. She *had* missed half her Lit classes — she'd developed a habit of slipping away to see Alyosha on Fridays. It was worth it.

The Americans gave away almost all their clothes and anything else they didn't need — disposable razors, books, cassette tapes, soaps, shampoos, and toiletries — to their Russian friends, who accepted them gratefully. Laura gave Nina her favorite sweater, two pairs of corduroys, and the five pairs of nylon stockings she'd been told to bring before she left. She wished she had more to give her, so she and Karen made a last-minute trip to the Berioska Shop for a jar of instant coffee, a tin of sardines, and some fancy chocolate.

Nina gave Karen and Laura each a copy of *Don Quixote* translated into Russian and a watercolor she'd painted of a church in her hometown in the Ukraine.

"I didn't know you could paint," Karen said. "It's very good, Nina."

Nina smiled shyly. "Thank you."

The painting was graceful and sweet: onion domes glittering in the summer sunshine, surrounded by leafy green trees. It showed a side of Nina that Laura hadn't noticed in the five months they'd lived together. There'd never been any evidence that Nina had ratted on Laura's bad behavior — at least, no one from the program had scolded her for staying out overnight and breaking so many rules. It was possible she'd somehow turned in Alyosha, but Laura didn't think so. She didn't think Nina knew who Alyosha was. Laura still didn't know how Alyosha had come to be arrested. It was one of the many mysteries of life in Leningrad.

"Thank *you*, Nina," Laura said. "And thank you for putting up with us."

"Oh, you are joking. . . ."

Laura was touched: Nina actually seemed choked up to see them go. And all this time Laura had thought Nina hated them.

"I hope you get that teaching job you want in Siberia," Karen added.

When Laura first heard that Nina was hoping to teach Spanish in Siberia, she thought it was absurd. She still thought · it was absurd, but after five months in the Soviet Union she no longer thought it strange. It made its own, weird kind of sense.

It was raining the day they left Leningrad. Laura rode through the city one last time on a bus headed for the airport, staring out the window at the pastel buildings set off against the gray sky, the gray river.

"I heard that if it rains when you leave town, that means someone is sad to see you go," Karen said. "It's an old Georgian superstition."

"I've heard that, too," Laura said. Roma had said it as they left the dacha. That weekend seemed far in the past.

At the airport they picked up their luggage and lined up to be inspected by Passport Control. For such a serious business, the actual, physical setup of the airport was pretty flimsy. Customs was divided from the waiting room by cardboard screens, and that was all. Passengers lined up in the waiting room, and when it was time for their luggage to be searched, an officer beckoned them to a table beyond the screen.

Laura had hidden Alyosha's painting — and Nina's, for it was illegal to take any art out of the country — in her luggage. Alyosha's fit nicely in a tampon box, surrounded by tampons. She hoped the customs officers would be too embarrassed to look closely in there. She'd rolled up Nina's watercolor and stuffed it in a pair of tights. She didn't want to lose either picture, but if they confiscated Alyosha's San Francisco icon, she'd be devastated.

The waiting room was crowded with passengers and people saying good-bye. In a corner, deep inside the crowd, Laura thought she spotted a familiar pair of sneakers. A babushka who was sweeping up dust moved out of the way and there he was: Alyosha. He kept behind the crowd, watching the group of Americans from a discreet distance.

He shook his head at her, ever so slightly, and she got the message: *Do not openly acknowledge my presence.* So she didn't. She gave him a sad smile, the tiniest smile, an ambiguous, Mona Lisa smile like the one he'd painted in his portrait of her.

He smiled back, also sadly. He raised one hand, almost a wave, but after holding his palm up to her for a split second, he rubbed his bare lip where the mustache once sat.

"Next!" a guard shouted at her. "Come on!" He waved her over to a table beyond the screen. Laura braced herself for the scrutiny.

Two men in uniform unzipped her suitcase and riffled through it. They patted the pile of tights without seeming to notice the paper hidden inside. They glanced at her school notebooks without catching the diary she'd shuffled among them. They opened the cardboard tampon box, peered delicately inside, and put it down.

She put away her things and zipped up her suitcase. She couldn't resist taking one last peek at the waiting room before boarding the plane.

She looked for Alyosha, but he was gone.

ACKNOWLEDGMENTS

Love and deepest gratitude to:

David Levithan, Becky Amsel, Erin Black, and everyone at Scholastic;

Sarah Burnes, Rebecca Gardner, Logan Garrison, Will Roberts, and everyone at the Gernert Company;

Rene Steinke;

Will and Betty Standiford;

and Alexander Ivanov.

Eric Weiner, I salute you.

About the Author

Natalie Standiford is the author of the acclaimed novels *How to Say Goodbye in Robot*, *Confessions of the Sullivan Sisters*, and (for younger readers) *The Secret Tree*. She grew up in Maryland, went to school in Rhode Island, and spent a semester in Leningrad during college. She now lives in New York City and can be found on the web at WWW.NATALIESTANDIFORD.COM.